ANIMAL
ALERT
QUARANTINE

Animal Alert series

1 Intensive Care
2 Abandoned
3 Killer on the Loose
4 Quarantine
5 Skin and Bone
6 Crash
7 Blind Alley
8 Living Proof
9 Grievous Bodily Harm
10 Running Wild

ANIMAL ALERT

QUARANTINE

Jenny Oldfield

Hodder
Children's
Books

a division of Hodder Headline plc

Special thanks to David Brown and Margaret Marks of Leeds
RSPCA Animal Home and Clinic, and to Raj Duggal M.V.Sc.,
M.R.C.V.S. and Louise Kinvig B.V.M.S., M.R.C.V.S.

Visit Jenny Oldfield's website at
www.testware.co.uk/jenny oldfield

Text copyright © 1997 Jenny Oldfield
Illustrations copyright © 1997 Trevor Parkin

First published in Great Britain in 1997
by Hodder Children's Books

The right of Jenny Oldfield to be identified as the Author
of the Work has been asserted by her in accordance with the
Copyright, Designs and Patents Act 1988.

British Library Cataloguing in Publication Data
A record for this book is available from the British Library

ISBN 0 340 68172 1

Typeset by Avon Dataset Ltd, Bidford-on-Avon, Warks

Printed and bound in Great Britain by
The Guernsey Press Co. Ltd, Guernsey, Channel Islands

Hodder and Stoughton
a division of Hodder Headline plc
338 Euston Road
London NW1 3BH

1

'Carly, please can you fetch Buster from reception?' Bupinda's voice came through on the intercom.

Liz Hutchins glanced across the treatment table and nodded at her. She was descaling the back teeth of an unconscious Yorkshire terrier. 'It's OK, I can manage here.'

So Carly rushed out of the treatment room to collect another patient.

'This is Buster.' Bupinda gave her a plastic pet carrier containing a small black cat. 'Be careful with him. He's just been found trapped under a car bonnet. We don't know how long he'd been there, but the car owner says she drove at least two miles without noticing.'

'Poor thing!' Carly took the carrier gently off the desk. The little cat was shivering, huddled in one corner.

'She heard a miaowing noise when she stopped at traffic lights. She had to hold up the traffic to get him out.' Bupinda picked up the phone to answer a call. 'Hello, Beech Hill Rescue Centre—'

Carly took Buster into the treatment room where her dad, Paul Grey, was based for morning surgery. It was empty when she went in, but he soon came in through another door.

'So, this is the cat who hitched a lift into town, eh?' He glanced at a card stuck to the front of the carrier. 'Buster? You don't look much like a Buster to me!' Lifting the cat out gently, he put him on the treatment table and began to examine him. 'No broken bones, one small burn on the tip of his left ear – Carly, can you find out if his owner's here?'

So she was off again, passing Melanie, the practice nurse, in the corridor.

'Carly, Steve just rang to say he's bringing in

an injured guard dog.' Mel caught her by the arm. 'Could you make sure the treatment table in the prep room has been wiped down, please?'

'Could you take these case notes upstairs to the filing cabinet, please, Carly!' Bupinda held up a folder from behind her desk.

'Help! How many hands have I got?' Carly dashed from room to room, up and down stairs, along spotlessly clean corridors. There was a queue of patients in the waiting room, a row of kennels full of hungry dogs all yelping to be fed.

'It's hot in here!' Mel complained as she dashed into the kennels. 'Have we got any room for the guard dog Steve's bringing in?' She checked the cages. 'Nope. Full up. Anyway, I expect it'll be a cruelty case. Steve will want it to be kept in isolation.'

'What happened?' Carly put food dishes in the cages, watching the dogs' tails wagging as they wolfed it down.

'Not sure. It's a Rottweiler. The security firm that owns it found it this morning. It had been attacked during the night. They called Steve. That's all I know.' Melanie stayed to help clear the empty bowls. 'He'll have to investigate, I expect.'

The news made Carly frown. Cruelty cases were always hard. It usually meant the animal was kept in isolation at Beech Hill for a long time, until the case had been looked into. It could take weeks. She wondered how badly hurt the dog was.

Then Ruby, the Beech Hill tortoiseshell cat, came padding downstairs from the Greys' flat. She rubbed against Carly's legs, reminding her that she too was hungry.

Carly picked her up and cuddled her. She thought of Buster's narrow escape from under the car bonnet with only a singed ear. 'Don't you go hitching any lifts, you hear!' she whispered softly. Ruby had already used up one of her nine lives when Carly had rescued her and the rest of her litter from a cardboard box dumped on a dual carriageway.

Ruby purred, until one of the dogs in the kennels spotted her. He jumped up at the wire-mesh door, barking madly. Ruby hissed back and leaped from Carly's arms. She shot out of the kennels, into the busy corridor, almost up-skittling Paul Grey.

'Have you seen Liz?' her dad broke into her thoughts.

'Not lately. Sorry.'

'Hey.' Liz happened to be passing. 'Did I hear my name mentioned?'

'Oh Liz, there you are. Bupinda has just taken a call-out case. I thought you'd like to take a look at it, since your background's with large animals.'

The assistant vet took a slip of paper from him. ' "Worsley Common Riding School", ' she read. 'What's the case?'

'A pony has flu, apparently.' Paul Grey checked his watch. 'We've nearly finished surgery here, so why don't you get straight off?'

Liz smiled, pleased to be trusted with the call-out. She'd come to work at Beech Hill from Scotland. Her family lived on a farm, which had made her want to train as a vet in the first place. 'Thanks. Where's Worsley Common?'

'I know!' Carly jumped in eagerly. 'It's out of town towards Sturminster!'

'Why don't you show Liz the way?' Paul suggested.

'Sure you don't need me here?' She didn't wait for an answer. Whipping off her plastic apron and running upstairs to the flat to feed Ruby, she was still ready in reception before Liz had even had time to collect her bag.

'Hello. I'm Trish Clarke.' The owner of Worsley Common Riding School, a tall woman with fair hair tied back, shook hands with Liz. 'Sorry to drag you all the way out here on a Saturday. I know how busy you must be.'

'That's OK. Sorry we took so long.' Liz was brisk and businesslike as they crossed the yard. 'The traffic was bad.'

Carly had used a map to guide them out of the city. Dual carriageway had given way to narrow, country roads. Worsley Common, a popular weekend picnic spot, was choked with traffic, the carparks bursting at the seams.

It was half past one on a sunny summer's day. The air was heavy with pollen, the drone of insects, the distant whine of traffic on the main road. Carly took in the drowsy atmosphere of the stable yard: doors swinging open, tack hanging from hooks inside a dark room, the sweet smell of hay.

'I don't suppose it's anything serious,' Trish Clarke was saying. She opened a stable door and stood to one side. 'Minty's been off her feed for a couple of days, and she's developed a bit of a cough.'

Liz listened and nodded. 'Sounds like flu. Hasn't she been vaccinated?'

The owner of the stables frowned slightly. 'That's just it. We've only had Minty for a few days. Her owners left her with us while they're on holiday.'

'And you didn't ask to see her vaccination certificate?'

'We're so busy, it must have slipped by.'

Liz shrugged. 'Easily done, I know.'

'We had all our own horses done in spring, of course.' Trish wanted to show that she ran her stables properly. She was embarrassed by the slip-up. 'Anyway, that's why I called you in to take a look as soon as I realised Minty hadn't had her flu jab.'

As they talked, Carly took in her surroundings. The yard did look neat and well-looked-after. The concrete surface had a drain running down the centre, plenty of water taps and nicely painted white doors. The stables were built around three sides of a square, with a cottage-style house set back in a garden full of bright flowers. But it seemed quieter than she'd expected: no horses gazing out over the half-open doors, and none in the field at the back of the house.

'The ponies are out on a hack in Minster Woods.' Trish picked up Carly's unspoken question. 'I'm expecting them back any time now. We've got a lesson at two-thirty.'

'Let's get on, shall we?' Liz suggested.

Carly followed her into the stable. 'Is flu serious?' she asked quietly, getting used to the shadows after the glare of the sun. Minty stood quietly in her stall, her head drooping. She was a dappled grey pony, with a long white mane and large, liquid brown eyes.

'Not usually.' Liz approached her patient calmly. She ran a hand down the pony's neck, her expert eye taking in every aspect of Minty's appearance. 'It can be nasty in young foals, but in a fully grown pony like this it's not much more than a high temperature and a nasty cough. In fact, it's sometimes called "the cough". The virus likes hot dry summers like this.'

Carly admired the confident way Liz had with the pony. She watched her feel for a pulse by placing her thumb against the bottom of Minty's cheek.

'It's a bit fast, but not much. Come and feel.'

Carly edged forward, aware of Trish Clarke hovering by the door. Though she wouldn't admit it, animals as large as Minty made her nervous. Dogs, cats, guinea pigs, terrapins – no problem. Horses, cows, anything big that lived in the country – that was a different matter.

'Come on, it's only because you're not used to it.' Liz showed her where to put her thumb. 'It should be forty beats per minute. Minty's is fifty. But it's nothing to worry about.' She grinned at Carly as she went round to the pony's rear end. 'Don't worry, I won't ask you to take her temperature!'

Carly smiled back. She could feel Minty's warm breath as she stood face to face, getting the feel of the pulse and trying her best to time it.

'Equine influenza. Horse flu.' Liz read the thermometer and confirmed that the pony's temperature was high. 'Just over a hundred.' She came alongside and sounded her chest with a stethoscope before she offered it to Carly. 'Take a listen. Can you hear that wheezing noise?'

Carly nodded.

'The flu virus attacks the tiny air sacs in the lungs and they get inflamed. That's what causes the cough.'

'Watch out!' Trish warned from the door. She'd seen Minty lower her head and stretch her neck. Suddenly there was a loud, wheezing, spluttering sound from deep in the pony's chest. She coughed, then shivered from head to foot.

'Just like human flu, really.' Liz decided what they must do. 'We need a rug to keep in her body heat. But you should leave the stable door open to let in the fresh air,' she told Trish. 'I'll give her a shot of antibiotics to stave off any secondary infection.'

'Will she be able to eat?' Carly helped fasten the special rug under the pony's belly. The poor thing stood miserable and listless, but seeming to understand that they were doing their best for her.

'A light bran mash only,' Liz instructed. 'Plenty of water, of course.' She finished the injection, then stepped back looking thoughtful. 'We could try steaming her if you like.'

The owner glanced at her watch, then over her shoulder at the procession of ponies and riders just visible along the lane. 'I haven't got time. I have to get these ponies ready for the lesson. A group of blind children come along every Saturday with their teachers from the special school at Fiveways.'

'That's OK, Carly and I will do it.'

'We will?' As the relieved owner went off, Carly hissed that she hadn't a clue what Liz meant by 'steaming' Minty. Still, she was willing to learn.

'Take this old feed bag and stuff it full of hay from that net.' Liz gave instructions. 'It's what we used to do on the farm when I was a kid. That's right. Now we need a bucket of boiling water.'

As Liz went off to sort this out, Carly spoke softly to the unhappy Minty. In the yard they could see the fit ponies stamping and snorting as their riders dismounted. Grey and brown, white and piebald, stout and sturdy or slim and elegant, they swished their tails and shook their heads to the tinkling of bridles and the creak of leather. The riders unsaddled them and brushed them down, led them off to drink, chatting all the while.

'Don't worry, you'll soon be out there with them again,' Carly promised. 'Flu's nothing. You'll be better before you know it.'

Minty hung her head. Beneath the heavy rug, she was still trembling.

Then Liz came back and poured the boiling water over the hay in the bag. She added a few drops of strong-smelling liquid from a small, dark bottle before she strapped the whole thing behind the pony's ears, letting the steaming feed bag hang loosely under her nose.

Minty breathed deeply. She took the steam in through her nostrils into her lungs.

'What did you put in there?' Carly asked. The liquid smelled strong and sickly sweet. She wrinkled her nose.

'Friar's balsam and oil of eucalyptus. It clears up the sinuses, makes it easier for her to breathe. It's good for her, see!'

Minty nipped at the hay as she kept on breathing in the medicine. She stamped her hooves dully on the bed of straw that lined the stable floor and whisked her tail. It was true: Liz's old-fashioned steaming trick seemed to be working.

They let the pony nibble at the hay and breathe

in the vapour until the steam stopped rising. Outside in the yard, Trish and her helpers were busy resaddling some of the ponies ready for the lesson. They ran about with bridles and bits, special leading reins and saddles for their disabled riders. Then, as parents drove off with the children who had been on the ride to Minster Woods, the school bus bringing the blind children to the lesson arrived.

'And we thought *we* were busy!' Liz remarked. She unhitched the feed bag from Minty's head and gave her one last check before they closed the stable door after them.

Carly smiled. She didn't know a thing about fetlocks and withers, hocks and pasterns. The strange names to do with horses were a mystery to a city kid like her.

But the atmosphere here at Worsley Common was friendly. She liked tall, wiry Trish Clarke and her no-nonsense manner. She liked the way everyone knew just what to do with the weird bits of leather and metal tack, and above all, she decided, she liked the smell, sight and sound of the ponies.

'Want to stay and watch?' Trish called, reading

Carly's mind as the children got slowly out of the bus.

2

'It's good for the kids and it's good for us,' Trish explained. She leaned her tanned arms along the top rail of the white fence, watching the helpers lead the ponies and their blind riders around the paddock.

Carly was surprised. She'd expected the riders to be nervous up there in the saddle. She knew she would be, and *she* could see! But they all sat easily, with straight backs, wearing hard hats and holding the reins as if they didn't have a care in the world.

'I can see it helps the kids,' Liz agreed. 'But I

would have thought it was expensive for you to have all these extra helpers on hand.'

Trish nodded. 'We get some volunteers, but we do have to pay extra staff. I don't like to charge the school too much, because it's run by a charity. So up till now, you're right, we haven't made much money on it.'

Carly watched as the lead pony changed direction and broke into a trot. The rest followed. The blind kids had good balance. She noticed that the beginners came at the end of the line, on ponies that were fat and slow. *That would be me*, she thought.

'Sophie, look out for Ginger!' Trish spotted a stout old pony take a nip at the rump of the one in front. 'We have to watch him,' she told Liz and Carly. The procession was leaving the paddock and heading up a track towards Minster Woods. 'Anyway, you could say it's paid off running the class without a profit for so long.'

Liz watched them go. 'How come?'

'I had some good news yesterday. We heard that we're to be given Lottery cash to develop Worsley Common as a riding school for special kids like these. We'll be able to expand, buy more equipment, pay more staff. It's a big boost for us.' Trish smiled and stood up straight. 'We're getting a visit from the Lottery people some time next week. If they're happy with what they see, the grant will go ahead.'

It was time to get on, Carly realised. She and Liz had to be back at the surgery for five, and Trish said she had stables to muck out while the ponies were out. So they glanced in at Minty before they left, then headed for town.

The radio was on, the soft top of Liz's ancient sports car was down and the wind was in their hair as they sped along the motorway. Before long, they could see the tower blocks ahead, and soon they were sweeping over Fiveways Junction, looking down on underpasses and housing estates, with the city centre before spread out them.

'Uh-oh.' Liz pulled off the motorway at the sign for Morningside. She stopped singing along with the radio. 'I just thought of something.'

'What?' Carly had shoved a baseball cap over her dark curls to stop the wind blowing her hair over her face. The car slowed down as they entered the snarled-up city traffic.

'I should have reminded Trish to keep Minty in isolation. Flu's infectious.'

'Don't worry. Everyone knows that.' In any case, Carly thought, each pony was kept in a separate stall.

'Yes, but I wish I'd made a point of it. With these Lottery people due to visit, she doesn't want half her horses to go down with the flu.'

'Ring her when we get back.'

'Good idea.' By now the traffic had slowed to a crawl. Liz tapped the steering wheel. 'It'd be quicker to walk,' she muttered.

So they arrived at Beech Hill only just in time for the beginning of surgery. There was already a queue in the waiting room, and an anxious-looking Bupinda at the desk.

'Oh, Liz, Paul says can you take the cat in room one?' The receptionist grabbed them as soon as they walked in. 'And Carly, Mel says can you hose down the kennels and the exercise yard? She's been too busy to do it this afternoon.'

They got to work, caught up in the hectic pace of yet another clinic. Liz put on her white coat and disappeared into the treatment room, while Carly went into the back to put on wellies and set the hose whooshing over the concrete yard at the back of the Rescue Centre.

'Hey, watch where you're spraying that!'

She looked up to see Hoody perched on the wall, his legs swinging down into the yard. She aimed the jet and got his trainers.

'Hey!' He leaped up and stood on the top of the wall.

'Sorry!' she grinned. 'Do you want to do something useful?'

'Depends.'

'Grab that brush and get sweeping.' Carly played the jet of water into the corners.

He jumped down and took the brush. 'Can I let Vinny in?'

'Yep, if he doesn't mind getting wet.' She was glad to see Hoody, but she wouldn't show it.

'Here, boy.' Hoody opened the gate and Vinny came bounding through the puddles. 'So where were you?' he asked.

Carly sprayed while Hoody brushed. She told him about the riding school and the special lesson for the blind kids, described the ponies, the stables, the weird names for tack. 'You've got bridles and bits, martingales and head collars, stirrup leathers and girths—'

'Great,' he grunted, head down, brushing the soapy water down the gulley. 'Like, I'm supposed to be interested in this?'

Carly stopped pointing the hose and glanced up. 'Why? Don't you like horses?'

The question made Hoody scoff. 'Listen, the only real live horse I've ever seen is at a football match, OK? And he's got this policeman on his back, and the two of them are shoving into the crowd, right?' He paused. 'Yeah, I like horses. I love 'em!'

This was a long speech for him, and it made Carly think there was something else behind it. She realised Hoody might be feeling left out. 'You could come with us next time.'

'Where to?'

'Worsley Common. We'll probably have to go back and visit Minty again some time soon.'

'Minty!' He curled his lip. 'What kind of a name is that?'

'What kind of a name is Vinny?' she retorted. Hoody's dog was a short-haired hotchpotch: brown-and-black stripes, with a white chest – a bit of bulldog, a lot of this and that.

Hoody didn't bother to answer. 'Minty!' he said again, mincing the word. 'Well, excuse me while I shorten his stirrup leathers and tighten his girth!' He mimed being a rider, using the broom handle as the horse.

' "Her"! Minty's a filly.' She knew she should never have corrected him the moment she opened her mouth.

Hoody flung down the broom. He glared at Carly, his eyebrows knotted, his mouth bunched and puckered. 'Great!' he said, striding towards the gate. 'Come on, Vin!'

He left without another word. The gate slammed, the jet from the hose splattered against it as Carly turned, too late to stop him.

'Tired?' Paul Grey asked Carly after the clinic had closed.

'A bit.' She was sitting in the office flicking through a book called *The Anatomy of the Horse* by Saunders and Cooper. She had her elbows on the desk, her chin in her hands. 'Diseases of the Leg: Bog Spavin, Boggy Hock, Thoroughpin, Windgalls'. It was like reading a foreign language.

Her dad glanced over her shoulder. 'I see you've got the horse bug.'

'Sort of.' She wasn't sure. She still kept thinking of Hoody being angry when she tried to get him interested. 'Dad—'

'Hmm?' He tapped at the computer keyboard, bringing a file up to date.

'You don't think liking horses is a bit kind of, well, snobby, do you?'

He paused to think. 'Well, you do need a fair bit of money if you're going to be a horsey sort of person. So I suppose, yes, you could say it's a snobby hobby!'

Carly thudded the book closed. 'That's what Hoody thinks.'

'Did he say that?'

'No. But I can tell.'

'Vets can't afford to be choosy about the type of owner we deal with,' Paul reminded her. 'Snobby or not, it's the animal that matters.' He looked round as Liz came in. 'Did you write up that case of equine influenza?' he asked.

Liz sighed and slumped into the nearest chair. 'Not yet. I just called the riding school. I meant to do it before the surgery, but I didn't get time.'

'And?'

'Trish Clarke says Minty's worse.'

Carly felt her interest in horses suddenly revive. 'Worse in what way?'

'She's coughing a lot more. And she won't eat. I said she'd better keep her away from the other horses.' Liz looked troubled as she got out of the chair and paced up and down the room.

'Would you like to run through it with me?' Paul's invitation was gentle.

Most people would want to go off duty and forget about work on a Saturday night, Carly thought. But not her dad. He was the best vet in the city; the best, full-stop.

'OK. I assumed it was flu because that's what the owner said it was, and that's what I was looking for.'

'Cough, fever, poor condition?'

She nodded. 'And the pony's flu jabs aren't up to date.' Liz thought of another reason to back up her diagnosis.

'But now you're not so sure?'

'I'm wondering what else it could be.' Liz listed the possibilities. 'Colic? No, I listened and there was no obstruction in the bowel. Some kind of food poisoning? Possibly. The pony was sweating, had poor appetite, rapid pulse.'

'Something in the hay that shouldn't be there, perhaps?' Paul listened carefully. 'But that would affect more than one pony in the stables, surely.'

Liz agreed. 'And we can rule out tetanus. The jaws weren't locked together, there was no stiffness in the legs.'

'Thank heavens for that.'

Carly knew that tetanus was one of the worst illnesses an animal could pick up. There was no cure and the patient usually had to be put down. So, thank heavens; she agreed with her dad. But she felt herself growing tense as, like painstaking detectives at the scene of a crime, Liz and her dad tried to pin down exactly what was wrong with Minty.

'You say you sounded her chest and there was a cough?' Paul picked up on one of the symptoms. 'Was it a dry cough or a wet one?'

There was a flicker of alarm in Liz's blue eyes. 'Wet,' she said slowly.

'Any mucus in the nose?'

Liz glanced at Carly and nodded. 'We tried friar's balsam to clear the sinuses.'

'Clear or yellow?' His voice grew quick, he shot the questions at his assistant.

'I can't say. I didn't pay enough attention.' Her pale complexion reddened. 'What are we saying – that I got it wrong?'

'We're saying we'd better go back and check.' He decided in a split second. 'But don't panic, this is just to make sure.' He invited Carly to come along, phoned Trish Clarke to say they were on their way, and got them out into the car, and driving towards Sturminster before she had time to think what getting it wrong might mean.

'I should have double-checked,' Liz muttered, pale now and angry with herself. 'The cough was wet. I should have taken that into account!'

'Don't worry, no one's right one hundred per cent of the time. Anyway, let's not jump to conclusions.' Paul checked his watch and looked at the red sunset over the rolling Sturminster hills. The journey had taken less than half an hour, so there would be time to examine the pony before dark.

'There's Trish.' Carly pointed to a figure standing at the gate as they drove down the last stretch of lane. She opened it to let them drive straight in, then led them to Minty's stable.

'How is she?' Liz stepped inside, followed by Paul and Carly.

'See for yourself.'

The answer was all too obvious. The pony stood shivering in her stall, her head hanging. She rolled her eyes at them as they went in, but seemed too weak to move. And running from her nose Carly could see something that hadn't been noticeable before: an ugly yellow discharge.

Paul Grey took one look. 'It's not flu,' he said quietly. 'What we've got here is a case of strangles.'

Carly wished she knew what the strange word meant. All she knew was that it was serious, very serious.

First her father felt the glands on the pony's neck to show Liz and Trish that they were swollen. 'You'll soon see abscesses forming here,' he warned. 'And possibly behind the ears too.'

'So you're absolutely certain?' Trish longed for him to change his mind. 'It's strangles?'

Carly wanted to leap in and ask, 'What is it?' but they were too busy to answer.

'Yes. It's definite. The first thing is to move all the other horses as far away as possible,' Paul instructed. 'Especially the youngsters. They're more likely to die from this disease, and it can spread like wildfire; you know that.'

Liz and Trish ran to move the horses out of the adjoining stables into the field at the back of the house, while Carly stayed to help her dad.

'Next, we have to muck out all this bedding, pile it into a heap in the yard and burn it.'

They seized rakes propped by the wall and began clearing the floor. The metal prongs scraped the concrete with a harsh rasping noise, unsettling the ponies across the yard.

As dusk fell, the whole stables grew edgy. Hooves clattered against wooden partitions, horses whinnied and shoved as they were led out to pasture.

'When we've got rid of every last scrap of infected straw, we have to disinfect the floor and the feeding equipment, then we have to position footbaths at every exit so that no one treads the infection away on their shoes.' Carly's dad told her to stand back as they finished heaping the bedding into a mound. Then he took a match and set fire to it. 'You stay to make sure it doesn't get out of control. I'll see you in a few minutes.'

As he vanished back into Minty's stable, Carly watched the flames crackle and catch. Soon they leaped high, twisting and flaring, then dying in a fountain of sparks in the dusk sky. She raked stray wisps of blazing straw back on to the heap, dodged the sharp smoke as it caught in her throat and stung her eyes.

When Trish and Liz came back into the yard, the flames were dying back into a smouldering pile of ash. For a while they stood and watched it in silence.

'We've done all we can for the moment.' Paul came out to join them. 'I've washed out Minty's nostrils and smeared them with Vaseline. You must make sure to steam her twice a day and watch for the abscesses to come to a head. Then call me back.' He took Trish to one side. 'It's got to be strict isolation from now on, I'm afraid.'

'For how long?' Her voice trembled.

Carly tried to see her face, but it was too dark. She listened instead with a sinking heart.

'Until we're sure there aren't going to be any more cases. Maybe two or three weeks. Do you want to inform the police and the Ministry, or shall I?'

Carly heard Trish gasp.

'The police?'

'Yes. Strangles is a notifiable disease. We have to do all we can to stop it from spreading.'

'But they'll close me down!' She turned away, then rushed towards Liz. 'You hear that? They're going to slap a quarantine notice on me and stop me from running my school! It's strangles, not flu!'

'I know. I'm sorry.' Liz backed away, unable to meet Trish's angry gaze. She stepped on to the edge of the bonfire, raising fresh sparks from the dying embers.

'Flu, you said!' Trish was shouting, waving her arms, wanting to hit out. 'My ponies could die here, my school's going to be closed down, thanks to your wrong diagnosis!'

Her voice broke. 'Sorry isn't enough!' she cried, running back to the house before they could stop her.

3

'How come it's Liz's fault?' The moment Hoody heard, he stuck up for her.

Carly had met up with him in the park at the back of the Rescue Centre. It was early Sunday morning, cool and fresh, with banks of white clouds in the sky.

'It isn't. But Trish thinks it is. Dad says it's because she's upset. She has to blame someone.'

They'd walked Vinny and a greyhound from the kennels, and now they were heading back to Beech Hill together. Hoody was nervy and off-hand, Carly uneasy after a restless night thinking about Minty. She wondered if they were going to have another row about nothing.

'If you ask me, it's Trish what's-er-name's fault.'

'How do you make that out?' Carly put the greyhound back in her kennel. She let out a litter of six-week-old, homeless mongrel pups to play in the yard.

'She said it was flu in the first place, didn't she?' Hoody lounged against the gate. 'You'd think she'd know what was wrong with her own horses.'

'Minty doesn't belong to Trish,' Carly told him. 'Her owners are on holiday. Anyway, it's still the vet's job to diagnose an illness.' She noticed Hoody stiffen and stand up straight. 'Well, it is! You can't just go by what the owner thinks is wrong—'

Hoody coughed and jerked his head in a look-behind-you gesture. Carly turned to see Liz standing quietly in the doorway.

'Oh! I didn't mean – I wasn't saying that it was your fault, Liz!' Carly felt her stomach knot up.

The young vet nodded. 'I know. You don't need to. I already blame myself. And you don't need to stick up for me either, Hoody. But thanks anyway.' She smiled faintly. Dressed in jeans and a white sweatshirt for her day off, she looked younger than her twenty-four years.

'Don't take any notice of this Trish woman,' Hoody insisted. 'You went back and sorted it, didn't you?' Carly had told him about the second visit – the disinfecting and burning, the quarantine notices.

'You can't "sort" strangles.' Liz went inside to look at a kennel separated from the rest. Nelson, the injured Rottweiler, lay quietly in one corner, recovering from his wounds.

'Why not? What's so bad about it?' Carly had followed her. She watched as Liz inspected the guard dog's stitches and took his temperature.

'Well, for one thing, we've left it late to vaccinate the other horses. A jab takes fourteen days to take effect. If they're going to catch it, it'll happen within the next forty-eight hours. In effect, Trish's entire stable is open to infection.' She stroked the dog, who lay with his cut and bruised head resting on his forepaws.

'So?' Hoody hovered in the door. 'Why's everyone going over the top about it?'

Liz stood up and backed out of Nelson's kennel.

'Strangles is a very painful disease. It's a strepto-coccus organism that attacks the lymph system.'

'What's that in English?'

'OK. You've got lymph nodes all over your body. Everyone has. So do horses. If you get abscesses on them, they swell up. If they're on the outside of the body and we can see them, we burst them and drain the pus—'

'Ugh!' Hoody curled his lip in disgust.

'You did ask! But if the abscesses are on the liver or the lungs, they burst and spread the infection inside the horse's body. That's when it gets really serious.'

'That isn't going to happen to Minty, is it?' Carly broke in.

Liz shrugged. 'It depends. The shot of anti-biotic I gave her yesterday on our first visit should help.' She paused and shook her head. 'Let's hope it was enough. Anyway, I promised your dad I'd go along with him this morning to check all the ponies for symptoms.'

As she went off to find Paul, Carly decided to twist Hoody's arm to come with them to Worsley Common.

She would have her work cut out, she knew. In

the city, Hoody was king. He knew the streets, the estates, the other kids. He wasn't part of any gang, never seemed to go home, liked everyone to think he was tough and hard. But she couldn't picture him in the country, without pavements, tower blocks, traffic.

'You'll like it. It's interesting,' she promised.

'I won't. I hate the countryside. There's nothing to do.' He hadn't stopped sulking, even though he'd listened hard to Liz's explanations about strangles.

'There is. There's loads to see. The ponies will be out in the field, and there'll be no one around because of the quarantine.'

'I hate fields. I get hay fever.'

She ignored him. 'Bring Vinny. He'll be able to chase rabbits and things. Loads of exercise.'

Hoody hesitated. He looked down at his tough, barrel-shaped dog. 'Are you saying he's fat?'

Carly grinned but said nothing.

'Admit it. That's what you're saying: Vinny's fat!'

'I said he'd like chasing rabbits.' She spread her hands. 'You were the one who mentioned the word "fat".'

'He's not fat,' Hoody muttered, stooping to stroke Vinny. 'Just well-built. Anyhow, I bet he could catch these rabbits, no problem.' He caught the challenge.

Carly heard her dad call her from reception. 'How will you ever know if you don't come with us?'

'Whose car are we going in?' Hoody demanded, his mind made up at last. He put Vinny on the lead and marched ahead. 'Come on, get a move on. What are we waiting for?'

Trish Clarke's riding school stood ghostly still and quiet. Stable doors hung open and a black heap of contaminated straw smouldered in the empty yard. The footbaths of disinfectant were in place.

'KEEP OUT!' Carly read the notice slapped on the gate. 'By Order of the Ministry of Agriculture, Fisheries and Food.' Underneath, in smaller lettering, was the warning about contagious diseases; no one was to enter or leave the premises except on official business.

'Are we official?' Hoody asked doubtfully. The notice brought home the dangers of spreading the deadly disease. He glanced down at Vinny. 'Can dogs catch it?'

'Yes, you're with us, so you're official. And no.' Paul Grey parked his car at the gate. 'It's a virus that only attacks horses, luckily. But I'd leave Vinny in the car in any case. We're going to have our hands full checking these ponies without him poking his nose in.'

Vinny yapped from the back seat.

'He wants a walk.' Hoody took the lead from his pocket. 'I'll take him up the hill first. See you later.' He loped off towards the woods, shunning advice, looking glum.

There was no time for Carly to worry about him. Trish Clarke had come out of one of the stables, carrying two buckets of steaming water, which she tipped and flung across the yard. She spotted Liz and deliberately turned her back to brush the flood into the drain, until Paul Grey approached to explain the regulations.

'We have to go ahead and vaccinate all the ponies. It may seem a bit late in the day, but that's what the rules say.' He said he was sorry about the way things had worked out.

Carly and Liz stood at a distance in the silent

yard. Liz looked as if World War III had started.

'Today's Sunday. It should be my busiest day.' Trish looked away. 'I've been ringing people since seven o'clock, telling them not to bother coming.' She talked wearily, as if she couldn't believe what had happened. 'The police came late last night, laid down the law about what I could and couldn't do. Basically, I can't let any of my ponies leave the property, and I can't let anyone in. It's like a prison!'

'How will you manage?' Paul walked with her towards the field, where the ponies were grazing.

'Badly,' she said with a hollow laugh. 'No lessons means no money coming in. And you know what the worst of it is?'

'Your visit from the Lottery people?' he guessed. 'Wasn't that supposed to be this week?'

Trish opened the gate and handed him a halter. ' "Was" is right. I can hardly invite them to come and look round a place that's just had a quarantine order slapped on it, can I? Anyway, I rang the special school this morning and told them what had happened. They said they'd be able to take the kids to another stables on the other side of town for the time being.' She shrugged. Carly noticed that her eyes were red round the rims, and there were shadows under them. 'So, I'll let you get on with what you have to do. I'll be in with Minty if you need me.'

She trudged off in her rubber boots, while Liz set about rounding up the ponies one by one. There were twelve in all, including the old bad-tempered one called Ginger and a young black colt who stuck nervously to his mother's side as Paul Grey gave each one in turn a jab.

'So far, so good,' he told them as they came to the end. They'd left the colt and old Ginger until last. 'As far as I can tell, none of these ponies has caught the disease.' He asked Carly to hold the young horse on a short lead while he injected the vaccine into his neck.

Nervously she did as she was told. The colt was young but strong. He didn't like the look of the needle and tried to shy away. His mother snorted and tossed her head, stamped her foot on a patch of worn earth.

'That's right, hold tight.' Paul concentrated on the injection.

Carly hung on to the rope and leaned against the pony to hold him steady. Between his pointed ears she caught sight of Hoody sitting on the fence watching. Vinny lay in the long grass beyond the fence, panting after his run through the woods.

Just before the needle went in, the colt reared up. He came down hard on Carly's foot. 'Ouch!' The pain shot up her leg.

'Steady!' Paul postponed the injection and took a quick look into the pony's mouth, then felt his pulse. He frowned and called Liz over. 'There's no point vaccinating him after all. I'm afraid we've got another case,' he told her.

They stood in a huddle, going over the colt's symptoms. Liz confirmed the worst. 'I'll go and find him an empty stable.'

'Are you sure you don't want me to do it?' Carly's dad asked.

'No. You finish here.' She led the colt off, coaxing him out of the field, away from his mother.

'Not good.' Paul shook his head and sighed. He sighed again once he'd examined Ginger. 'Another one,' he told Carly. He let her listen to the pony's laboured breathing. 'Better get him out of here,' he told her, 'and I'll go and give Trish the bad news.'

*

'Don't push from behind!' Carly warned.

Hoody stood at the entrance, trying to get the stubborn old ginger pony through the door. He'd put Vinny in the car and shown up to help when he heard Paul Grey diagnose two more cases of the deadly disease.

'See!'

Ginger lashed out with his hind feet, missing Hoody by inches. Hoody had sidestepped just in time. 'I hate horses!' he muttered.

'No, you don't. Look, we've got to get him in here before he infects all the others!' Carly was sweating with nerves. She could see Trish standing in the stable yard deep in conversation with her dad, her head hanging, her shoulders slumped. The strong-willed pony was still refusing to budge.

But now there was a look on Hoody's face, and he slid down the gap between Ginger and the doorpost. Shoving Carly to one side of the stall, he dipped in his pocket and held out his hand, palm flat, tempting him forward.

The pony inched suspiciously towards his hand, Hoody backed off. Again. And again. Then, as soon as Ginger was well and truly inside the stable, Hoody let him snatch the reward, vaulted sideways over the wooden partition, and ran and closed the door behind him.

'What was that you gave him?' Carly gasped in surprise.

'Doggy choc!' Hoody shot her a grin of triumph. 'It's a battle of wills, see? And you know you're never going to win. So you have to use your brain instead.' He was pleased with himself, leaning over to pat the pony's neck.

'Since when were you an expert?' She wished she'd thought of it before Hoody.

'Since one minute ago. It works for Vinny, so I figured, why shouldn't it work on a pony?'

They now had the three sick horses safely inside. Liz was already working with Spider, the black colt, so Carly and Hoody went to join Paul Grey in Minty's stable. What they found there soon dampened their spirits again.

Carly's dad had his shirt sleeves rolled back and was pressing a pad of steaming cloth against the abscesses on the grey pony's neck. Minty's nose streamed with foul mucus, her eyes were dull, her whole body shivering. 'I know,' he murmured as he worked. 'It hurts. You feel lousy. We're doing everything we can.'

He glanced up and asked Carly to stand by with a syringe. 'I'm nearly ready to lance this one,' he explained. 'And Hoody, take that feed bucket out into the yard, wash it and disinfect it, will you?'

Carly steeled herself to help with the unpleasant job. 'Is she getting worse?' It seemed to her that Minty's breathing was shallower, wheezier than before.

'Well, she's certainly no better. It'll be another few days before we'll know for sure.' He pointed out more swollen glands behind her ears. 'The infection's travelling. That's not a good sign,' he warned. He finished with the syringe and went to scrub his hands in a bucket in the yard.

'As for these two new patients,' he called in as the sound of a car engine approached down the lane, 'They're bound to keep us busy as well!'

The car stopped at the gate. *Probably pupils arriving for a lesson*, Carly thought. *They can't know about the quarantine*. A door slammed, she heard voices: Trish Clarke's and a stranger's.

'Hang on, what's going on?' her dad muttered.

She peered out over the stable door. There was a woman and a girl of about her own age arguing with Trish. Liz and Hoody had heard the raised voices and had come to look. Her dad walked across to where the argument was taking place.

'What do you mean, we can't come in and see her?' The woman had begun to shout.

Trish pointed at the KEEP OUT! notice.

'But Minty belongs to us. She's our pony!'

Quietly Carly followed her dad. The visitors had arrived in a big four-wheel drive. Mother and daughter were both small and slight, with long dark hair.

'We came back from our holiday specially to see her as soon as we heard she was ill! Julia's worried sick!'

'Mrs Mitchell, I'm terribly sorry. I can't let you in.' Trish stood her ground with a grim face.

'That's right.' Paul Grey backed her up. 'Strangles is so contagious that you could carry it away on the soles of your shoes. That's why we've placed these footbaths at the gate, so we can disinfect our shoes when we come and go. But we must keep movement to a minimum.

There's a good reason behind the quarantine regulations, believe me.'

'So what are they doing there?' Mrs Mitchell demanded. She pointed at Carly and Hoody.

'Helping,' Paul Grey said, unruffled and firm. 'There's a lot of work to do, mucking out and disinfecting twice a day. If we're going to save your pony's life, we have to do everything by the book.'

For a moment the woman backed off. Her daughter had begun to cry.

'If we break the rules and the infection spreads internally, your pony will die,' he insisted.

Carly held her breath and frowned. What would the woman do now? She heard the daughter sob loudly.

'This is terrible!' Half-frightened, half-angry, Mrs Mitchell turned on Trish. 'It's all your fault. We leave Minty with you while we go away, and we come back to find her at death's door! What kind of place is this?'

'Mrs Mitchell—' Paul Grey tried to step in. 'The incubation period for this disease is longer than seven days. Minty had probably caught it before you brought her here.'

But Carly knew the woman wouldn't listen. The girl cried, the mother yelled, Hoody scowled, Liz hung her head and Trish went pale. Five faces, all shocked.

'That's nonsense! It's this stable that's to blame. It needs reporting for being unfit to keep horses. Yes, that's it, you should be reported!' Mrs Mitchell wagged her finger in Trish's face.

'Mrs Mitchell—' Paul Grey said again.

'No, why should I listen to you? You're on her side, obviously.' She confronted Trish for one last time. 'If you don't let Julia see her pony, I'll have to go and make some phone calls.'

Silence. They stood helpless under the official notice.

The woman's eyes blazed, then she turned on her heel and made for her car. 'Right, I'm going to speak to someone in authority.' She ordered her daughter into the car and climbed up after her. Before she slammed the door shut, she issued her final threat. 'You'll see, I'm going to get you closed down for good!'

4

'I've had a Mrs Mitchell on the phone,' Steve Winter told them when they arrived back at Beech Hill.

It wasn't even lunch-time, and Carly already felt tired out. The news he gave them made her wearier still. 'What did she want, as if we didn't know?'

Paul Grey had already told Liz to go home for a rest on her day off. Hoody and Vinny had drifted off somewhere, so the Rescue Centre was deserted except for Carly, her dad, and their inspector. Steve Winter had worked at Beech Hill for a couple of years now. He'd left his job working on building sites to train in animal welfare. He was a softly spoken but firm man who drove their van to the scenes of accidents and investigated reports of cruelty. It was also part of his job to serve summonses for suspected owners to appear in court.

'She's reported Worsley Common Riding School for neglect,' he signed. 'I'll have to look into it, I'm afraid.'

Carly knew it was no good trying to put him straight. When he got a call from a member of the public, he had to follow it up. She trailed after him into the kennels, where Nelson the Rottweiler was recovering from his injuries. 'Was Mrs Mitchell still mad?' she asked.

'You could say that. Mind you, the Mitchells have had a shock. Coming back from holiday to find quarantine notices stuck up and your pony hovering on the brink between life and death can't be easy.' He told her that he would have to visit the stables later that afternoon. 'Now, on the other hand, I'm glad to say that Nelson here is certainly going to live to see another day!'

Carly stroked the dog's neck. Nelson wagged

his stumpy tail and thrust his soft muzzle against her hand. 'What's the story?'

'Another incident to do with ponies, funnily enough. You know the City Farm at Sedgewood?'

She nodded. 'We went with school when we were in Year 6.' Sedgewood was on the other side of town. The City Farm kept sheep, goats, pigs and other farmyard animals, as well as donkeys and ponies that children could ride.

'Well, apparently there'd been a couple of suspicious characters hanging around there for a day or two, looking as if they were up to no good. Some of those animals are fairly valuable, so the farm manager called in a security firm to keep a check on the premises at night.'

'And they set Nelson to guard the farm?' She knew that Rottweilers made ideal guard dogs, with their fierce, deep bark and strong, muscular bodies.

'Yep. And sure enough, there was an attempt at a break-in during the first night he was there. Geoff Best, the farm manager, reckons the thieves were after the ponies. Of course, they wouldn't be expecting a greeting from Nelson here. He did his job and saw them off, but not before they'd had a go at him.'

Carly flinched. 'What did they hit him with?'

Steve shrugged. 'Some kind of heavy metal bar by the look of it. When Geoff Best found him next morning, he was unconscious and he'd lost a fair bit of blood. Geoff notified the security firm then rang me. Poor chap, he only just made it.'

She made a fuss of Nelson now, telling him what a good, brave dog he was. Vicious cruelty like this made her blood boil. 'Did they catch the people who did it?'

'No. They vanished without trace. All we've got to go on is Geoff Best's description of the two suspicious men hanging around earlier in the week. One in his thirties, about six feet tall, well-built, with a dark moustache. One much younger, not much more than a kid, dressed in a black leather jacket.'

'They should be locked up,' she muttered, closing the door on Nelson to leave him in peace and quiet.

'Well, there's one thing for sure: I'd rather be spending my time chasing up criminal types like that than investigating Trish Clarke,' Steve agreed. 'As if she didn't already have enough to deal with!'

'I'm ruined.' Trish stood in the yard watching Steve check the stalls where she kept the infected ponies. She was hunched inside a green padded jacket, her face was pale and strained. 'One minute we're set to get a grant to help us expand, next minute I've got quarantine notices plastered everywhere and I'm being prosecuted for neglect!'

It was Sunday evening and Carly had persuaded Hoody to come back to Worsley Common with them. This time he'd left Vinny behind at his sister's house on Beacon Street.

'Only because I want to see how that ginger horse is getting on,' he'd insisted.

'Pony,' Carly had corrected him.

'Whatever.' He'd glared and shoved his hands in his pockets. 'And I don't want a lecture, either.'

Anyway, he was here, and they were mucking out Minty's stall for Trish, along with a helper called Sam, a mousy-haired girl of about eighteen who worked at the stables part-time. Minty looked just the same as earlier that day; dull-eyed and listless, with the ugly swellings by her cheeks and ears.

'I've reached the end of my tether,' Trish told Steve. 'There's the worry of it, and all the nursing. We have to disinfect the stalls three times a day, and steam the sick ponies as often as we can.

'I'll do that!' Hoody offered, sticking his head out of the stable. 'Whatever it is.'

'You won't like it,' Carly warned. She showed him the old feed bags hanging inside an empty stable, explained what they had to do, then went off to fetch a bucket of boiling water. 'And neither will Ginger.'

They went across the yard with the equipment they needed, leaving Sam to set fire to the soiled bedding. The smell of burning straw drifted across to them on the evening air as they worked with the stubborn old pony.

'OK, you hook the bag around his ears,' Carly began. She'd poured the water and the friar's balsam over the hay in the bag.

Hoody squeezed between Ginger and the closed door. He fumbled and fiddled with the straps. 'Which bit goes where?'

The pony wasn't about to let him find out. Instead, he took a nip at the bag and tossed the hot hay about, stamping his feet dangerously near to Hoody's trainers.

'Hey, watch it!' Hoody dodged. The pony shuffled sideways, trapping him against the stall. 'How do I get this thing on?' he cried.

Carly grinned. Obviously, being ill hadn't improved Ginger's temper. From where she was standing outside the stall, she saw him roll his eyes and shake his head.

'OK!' Hoody grew equally stubborn. He worked out the straps and approached the pony once more. 'This is for your own good, you stupid horse!' Quickly he slung the steaming bag around Ginger's neck.

'Oh yeah, he's bound to do as he's told if you sweet talk him!' Carly grinned again.

'He needn't think he's getting away without having this done.' Hoody ignored her and concentrated on tightening the straps so that Ginger breathed in the medicine. At last, the awkward patient gave in and stood quiet. Hoody was covered in bits of hay, his face was red and sweating, but he'd won.

'Now it's Spider's turn,' Carly told him, leading the way again.

The young colt was in a far worse state than tough old Ginger. They found him isolated from his mother, shut in a dark stall, looking poorly and miserable. He didn't resist as Carly fixed the feed bag around his nose. She could see the swollen abscesses behind his cheeks, noticed that his whole body was covered in sweat. She stroked him gently as he breathed in the steam, then she and Hoody mucked out the straw bedding as quickly as they could, to leave him in peace.

'Spider's pretty sick,' Sam told them. She piled more bedding from Ginger's stall onto the bonfire. 'His throat's so swollen he can hardly swallow.'

Carly stepped back from the smoke as the wind changed direction and her eyes began to smart. 'Either Dad or Liz will be here first thing in the morning,' she promised.

Sam sighed. 'I'm worried about Trish as well. She's not stopped once today, not even for a cup of tea. She's disinfecting everything in sight, and she keeps going out to the field to check the other ponies. She thinks they're all going to go down with this horrible strangles. She can't rest for thinking about it.'

There was nothing Carly could say to make it better. With three ponies sick from a highly infectious, deadly disease, a quarantine notice, and now an investigation by Steve, Trish Clarke certainly had plenty to worry about.

It was dusk when Steve called to tell them it was time to go. 'I want to drive round the back of the field to check the notices are in place all the way round. We don't want anyone trespassing from that far side.' He pointed to a track that ran out of Minster Woods and cut along the back of Trish's field. Then he turned to say goodbye. 'Try not to worry about the investigation,' he told her. 'As far as I can see, Mrs Mitchell doesn't have any evidence that you were deliberately neglectful. I'll make a report to the police, and my advice will be that no action needs to be taken.'

Trish nodded wearily. 'Thanks. Let's hope that will be enough to satisfy her.'

They left her and Sam, and drove down a tractor lane by the side of the field where the rest of the ponies grazed quietly in the evening sun.

No one felt like talking as they passed the quarantine warnings, posted every fifty metres, hanging from the white fence posts.

'OK, I don't think anyone can miss them.' Steve decided to turn back. He reversed the van up a grassy slope.

'Hang on, there's a way on to the road if you keep going straight on,' Hoody urged. 'The track meets up with it by the edge of the wood.'

So Steve changed his mind and drove on. They skirted the bottom of Minster Woods, driving through the deep shadow of the wooded slopes rising to their right as they bumped along the track.

'Car coming!' Carly warned. The oncoming Land-Rover and trailer were partly hidden by a bend.

They pulled off the narrow track to let it pass.

'Good job I stopped!' Steve frowned as the Land-Rover careered towards them. The trailer it was towing bounced and swayed, filling the whole track. The two men in the car didn't even slow down.

'What are they doing?' Carly choked on exhaust fumes as the car and trailer rattled past.

'This track doesn't lead anywhere except to Trish's place.'

'Probably farmers taking a short cut.' Steve set off without a second thought. 'The traffic's bad out here,' he grumbled as they joined the road. 'Everyone's heading for home at once before it gets dark.'

But Carly thought it was odd. The men in the Land-Rover didn't look like farmers. City types, definitely. She turned and glanced back at the stables. The house nestled at the bottom of the hillside, tiny from this distance. She could see a red glow of bonfire, the blobs of white, brown and black that were the ponies grazing in the field. It looked still and quiet; there was no sign of the Land-Rover that had been in such a hurry.

'What I wouldn't give for a good curry with hot lime pickle!' Steve sighed, as they joined the crawl of traffic heading into the city.

Nelson was well enough next morning for Carly to take him for a walk in Beech Hill Park. A damp drizzle kept most people indoors, so she strode out across the deserted football pitches and sat alone on a bench by the children's swings while the dog followed interesting scents in the grass.

A boy delivering newspapers cycled by, cap pulled well down, his bright orange bag sagging with the weight of his papers. Two smartly dressed women crossed the park briskly, heading for work. Then Hoody showed up out of the blue with Vinny in tow.

'I thought I'd find you here. Did you listen to the news?' he asked. He was out of breath, about to make a big announcement.

'No. Why?' She stood up and turned up her jacket collar to keep out the wet.

'You mean you haven't heard? Didn't your dad say anything?'

'I haven't seen him this morning. He was called out on an emergency before I got up. Come on, Hoody, if it's that important, just tell me.' She went to fetch Nelson and put him on the lead.

'It was on the national news, not just the local radio. Zoe had the telly on and I heard it with my own ears. Otherwise I wouldn't have believed it.' He drew breath, steadied himself. 'Last night someone broke into Trish's field and stole a pony!'

'You're kidding!' Carly felt like she'd been

kicked in the stomach. 'Tell me you are!'

He shook his head. 'It's true. They put it out on the main news because of the quarantine thing. They said this stolen pony could be a carrier of the disease. It spreads like wildfire, they said. They told the thieves they'd broken a strict quarantine law.'

' "Thieves"?' Carly gasped. 'How do they know there was more than one?' She'd begun to run with Nelson towards the Rescue Centre.

'Don't ask me. I only know what I just heard.' Hoody followed her across the park. 'The news reporter dragged in this expert. She said it was a killer disease. According to her, without even realising it, the stupid idiots that stole the pony have probably started a national epidemic!'

5

'Let's just deal with what we can!' Back at Beech Hill, Liz spoke with the voice of common sense.

The local and national newspapers were on the phone, bombarding Bupinda with questions for Steve about the stolen pony. Wasn't the riding school under investigation? Hadn't Trish Clarke already lost a huge Lottery grant? Was it true that she'd put children from a special school at risk?

The rumours ran wild, but, for the moment, Steve wasn't giving any answers. He and Carly's dad were in the office talking to two police officers, telling them everything they knew. Mel was at the main entrance explaining that morning surgery would be for emergencies only, while Liz laid out practical plans for the day.

'I'm going straight out to Worsley Common,' she told Carly. 'The break-in last night doesn't alter the fact that we still have three very sick ponies to look after. They'll need another shot of antibiotics, and all the usual nursing care.'

'Can I come?' Carly pleaded. 'I could stay to help Trish and Sam.

'And me,' Hoody offered.

'Better not.' Liz grabbed her bag and her car keys. 'The police might want to talk to you after they've finished in the office.'

'What for?' Hoody jumped as if he'd been standing on hot coals. He wove in and out of the patients waiting in reception, following Liz as she made for the door.

'You were there with Steve last night, weren't you? They might want to ask you if you noticed anything unusual.'

'I'd be more use if I came to Worsley Common,' he insisted.

'Hoody, no!' Liz told him once and for all. She

was gone, out of the main door without glancing round.

Carly watched him sag. He sneaked a look at the office door, then sloped off across the carpark with Vinny. It was the word 'police' that had done it. She knew they wouldn't be seeing Hoody again until the coast was clear.

He left just in time. Before he'd turned the corner on to the street, Steve opened the office door and beckoned her. There was a buzz of gossip in the waiting room at the sight of two dark blue uniforms beyond the door.

'Carly, can you come in here a minute?' Steve said quietly.

She went in nervously. Everything was strange: normal surgery had been cancelled, and even her dad was looking strained and worried.

'What I can't understand is anyone being stupid enough to ignore the KEEP OUT! notices.' Paul Grey sat at his desk, running a hand through his brown hair. 'I mean, anyone with a grain of sense would realise that even setting foot in that field was dangerous.'

'Maybe the thieves know nothing about this disease,' one of the policemen suggested.

'They can read, can't they?' Carly's dad snapped back. 'Any idiot knows what KEEP OUT! means!' He sighed and apologised. 'Sorry. But the signs do say that strangles is lethal to horses and that it's highly contagious. I just can't understand why anyone would ignore that!'

'And you're sure they would have seen the notices?' The other policeman asked Steve.

'Yes. What makes it even more difficult to believe is that all of these ponies have been freeze-marked.' He drew some papers out of a file on the desk. 'Here's a list of serial numbers. Trish Clarke gave it to me yesterday to keep my records up to date.'

'And these freeze marks can't be removed?'

'No, that's the point. Owners have a sort of permanent tattoo put on the horses; it's meant to deter thieves.'

The policeman took the list and read it through. 'The stolen pony is a black-and-white one called Smudge. Here it is.' He jotted down the serial number and gave the list back to Steve. 'This could be useful. We'll be able to notify other police forces, just in case the thieves travel with the stolen pony and try to sell it out of the area.'

He turned to Carly. 'We've been asking Steve here if he noticed anything unusual at the riding school last night.'

'And I couldn't think of anything.' Steve frowned as he put the paper back in the file. 'We were all pretty shattered by the time we'd finished. It had been a lousy day all round.'

'What about you?' The policeman spoke kindly to Carly. He was quite old and heavy, with slicked-back grey hair.

She shook her head. 'I was busy with the ponies. I saw a few people come up to the gate to read the notices, but they all went away again.'

'What sort of people?'

'Families. They looked like they wanted to book a lesson, then realised they couldn't.' Carly racked her brains. 'One or two people were hanging around for a bit, like they had nothing better to do.'

'But no one who looked suspicious?' The policeman wanted to make sure.

'No – except –' She paused.

'Except what?'

'When we were leaving – there was that Land-Rover!' She turned suddenly to Steve. 'You remember: the one with the trailer, on that track by the woods!'

'The farmers.' He nodded and shrugged. 'They nearly mowed us down. No consideration for townies, these farmers.'

But Carly wouldn't let him pass it off. 'I didn't think they looked like farmers.'

'What *did* they look like?' the policeman urged. 'Could you give me a description?'

'Not really. I just know they didn't seem how you think farmers should be.' She struggled to remember the glimpse she'd had of the two men. 'The one in the passenger seat was young. He had light hair, not really blond though. It kind of flopped over his forehead.'

'What about the driver?'

'Older. Dark hair, with a moustache.'

'What were they wearing?'

She hesitated. This was more difficult. She'd only had a moment to see. 'The young one had a leather jacket on!' The second she opened her mouth, she realised what it might mean. She gasped and turned to Steve. 'Leather jacket! You told me that's what one of those men who were hanging about Sedgewood City Farm was wearing!'

Steve came out from behind the desk, her dad asked her to explain, the two policemen hung on every word.

With all eyes on her, Carly stammered out her theory. 'I don't know why I didn't think of it earlier. I knew there was something odd, but I just didn't put the two things together.'

'Take it easy, Carly,' Paul Grey insisted. 'Tell us exactly what you're saying.'

So she took a deep breath and spelled it out. 'There were two men behaving suspiciously at Sedgewood last week. That's why they put Nelson on guard. They were probably the ones who attacked him and then ran off.'

Steve nodded and confirmed that this was true.

'Going by the description, what I'm saying is that they are still in the area, looking for another horse or pony to steal.'

'Professional horse thieves? And they picked Worsley Common?' Her dad stood up, scraping his chair, then strode around the room. 'What do you think?' he asked Steve.

'We know they're ruthless.' The inspector reminded them about Nelson's injuries. 'And if

Carly's right, they seem to fit the description Geoff Best gave us.'

'You are sure about this?' Paul asked her. 'You're not just wanting it to be true and imagining it? You only had a quick look, remember.'

Carly screwed up her eyes, tried to concentrate. The dark moustache, the sturdy figure hunched over the wheel, the sneering grin on the face of the young one with the leather jacket. 'It's true,' she insisted quietly. She felt convinced that the men who had battered Nelson were the ones who had stolen Smudge.

'We still have a Rescue Centre to run, remember!' Paul Grey was arranging the order of the surgical operations he had to carry out that afternoon. 'I can't drop everything to play detective with you, Carly. And neither can Steve.'

'That's what the police are for.' Steve had to spend the afternoon giving evidence in court against a greyhound trainer accused of drugging his dog's food. The tests had come out positive and the suspect had been arrested.

Carly nearly cried with frustration. 'But it feels like my fault! If I'd thought about it properly last night and realised who the men in the Land-Rover were, Smudge would never have been stolen. There wouldn't be all this panic!'

All morning the phone had rung. Liz had come back from Worsley Common, saying it was even worse out there. The press were camped out at Trish's gate, taking photographs every time she showed her face.

'Listen to me.' Her dad took her upstairs to the flat, sat her down, made her listen. 'None of this is your fault. In fact, you've given the police a good lead to follow up. Because of what you were able to tell them, they now know the make of car they should look for and the type of trailer, as well as the two suspects.' He waited for her to calm down. 'You have to realise you can't solve every problem we come across,' he said gently. 'And this one is much too big for us to handle.'

'But they must be somewhere!' She tried to picture what two men would do with one scared black-and-white pony. 'They can't have vanished into thin air!'

'Not our problem,' her dad insisted. 'Leave it to the police.'

'I can't stop thinking about it, Dad! I'm trying

to imagine what I would do if I was them. They must know everyone's after them. Even if they didn't realise beforehand what stealing a pony from that field would mean, they must have listened to the radio or seen the TV news by now!'

Sighing, Paul Grey got up from the sofa and went to gaze out of the window. 'OK, they don't have many options. For a start, the freeze mark means they can't sell Smudge legally to new owners.'

'Why not?'

'Because he's now on the register of stolen animals. And anyone buying a pony from a legitimate source would automatically check the register.' He glanced uneasily at Carly. 'So that's out. The same goes for trying to export him to new owners abroad. All the ports have the same list of stolen ponies. They wouldn't let the trailer on to a ferry.'

'What are you trying to say?' It seemed that the thieves must be driving up and down the country, desperately trying to find someone who would buy Smudge without asking too many questions.

'I'm saying there are only two other things I can think of.' Paul Grey went and sat next to her again. 'First, they could just dump the pony where nobody can see them doing it. They might think good riddance after the panic it's caused. But that, of course, puts every other horse and pony in the area at risk of being infected with strangles.'

'Do you think they will?' Poor Smudge – dumped and scared.

'No. I think it's more likely they'll still try to make a bit of money out of him.' Paul presented her with the last option. 'You're going to hate this, Carly, but the fact is that most stolen ponies don't live for very long after they've been taken.'

'Why not? What do you mean?' Her voice caught in her throat, her mouth went dry.

'Because a thief will know, when all else fails, he can still get paid a certain amount of money if he takes the animal to a slaughterhouse.' He held her hand and broke it to her. 'The thief pockets the money and the pony's put down. And in this case – given the circumstances – considering that the quarantine's been broken – well, the slaughterhouse might be for the best.'

'Oh!' Carly jumped up, speechless. She put her hands over her ears, wished that her dad had never spoken those words.

'Carly, wait!' Paul ran after her as she dashed for the door and downstairs, through reception. 'Stop her, Mel!'

But Carly pushed past the nurse and flung herself through the door. Through eyes blurred with scared, angry tears, she saw Hoody sitting with Vinny under a tree on the wall across the street.

He jumped down when he saw her run out. 'Watch it!' he yelled.

A car had to brake suddenly as she ran across the road. Its tyres squealed on the wet surface.

'Are you coming or not?' she demanded, brushing the hot tears away with the back of her hand. She pretended it was rain on her face.

'Where to?' He could tell that it wasn't rain, but he didn't let on.

'Worsley Common,' she shot back at him. 'On the bus.'

'I take it your dad doesn't know?' He followed her to the stop on City Road.

'I'll ring him when I get there.' She wanted

Hoody's help, but she had no time to stop and explain. A bus was on its way, slowing down at the stop. The door hissed and folded open.

They scrambled on with Vinny and sat down near the front. 'Why are we doing this?' Hoody demanded.

Carly forced her jumbled thoughts into order. He didn't know anything about the tangled connection between Nelson and Smudge. As the bus lurched out into the traffic, she began at the very end of the story so far.

'Because we have to do *something*!' she told him. 'Because Smudge is going to end up as dog meat if we don't!'

6

Carly and Hoody found Trish Clarke and her helper, Sam, in the yard at Worsley Common. They were scrubbing and disinfecting feed buckets, too busy at first to stop and listen to Carly's story.

'Not you again,' Trish muttered. She glanced at Vinny and told Hoody to keep him on the lead. 'Can't you see we're up to our eyes in it?'

'Spider's worse,' Sam explained. 'Liz came this morning and said it looks like the abscesses have spread. He won't eat because of his throat, and now he's too weak even to stand.'

'How about the other two?' Hoody asked, while Carly went to peep at the sick colt.

'They're holding their own. They can take a bit of soft mash, and they're drinking plenty. Liz lanced the abscesses, so they're not in so much pain.' Sam stopped work as Carly came back. 'See?'

She nodded. 'Poor thing.' Spider was lying on his side, the ridges of his ribcage showing, his skinny legs stretched out. He hadn't even raised his head when she peered in.

Trish worked on. She dipped grooming bushes in a strong solution of disinfectant with hands reddened from water and hard work. 'That young vet of yours is doing her best, I'll give her that,' she said grudgingly. 'Even if she did make the wrong diagnosis in the first place, she's making up for it now.'

'So what did you want to know?' Sam changed the subject. 'It must be pretty important for you to come out here on the bus.'

Hoody spoke for Carly. 'Did anyone see those two men with the trailer yesterday afternoon? The ones we've just told you about!' Carly had spilled out a description the moment they'd arrived, told them how ruthless the thieves were, how they'd already tried to steal ponies from the City Farm.

'What time exactly?' Sam tried to be helpful. She smiled sympathetically at Carly, who was still shocked by the sight of Spider.

'Late afternoon. We want to know if they were hanging about, waiting for it to get dark.' Hoody kept his mind on the facts, hoping to pick up anything that would help.

'Maybe.' Sam was thoughtful. 'I did hear my brother mention something a bit weird when he came home from The Rose and Crown last night. He works behind the bar,' she explained. 'Rob said there were a couple of men in around tea-time, trying to sell a Land-Rover and trailer. They asked him if he knew whether anyone would be interested.'

'Why did he think that was weird?'

'Because they weren't local. No one had ever seen them before so everyone was going, "No way!" Rob thought the stuff was probably nicked.'

'So what did the men do?'

'According to Rob they went off as soon as

someone mentioned legal stuff like MOT certificates. They shot out of the carpark and that was the last anyone saw of them.'

'What time?'

Sam shrugged. 'I didn't ask. Oh, there was one other thing. When Carly mentioned the City Farm, the penny started to drop. Apparently, the men said they were from the Sedgewood area and that's where the Land-Rover had come from. It's a dodgy area, so that was another reason why no one in the pub was interested in doing business with them!'

'So – they went off from the pub, gave up on making money out of the Land-Rover, came here and stole Smudge instead.' Carly managed to put her fears about Spider to one side. She began to think things through. 'If they came from Sedgewood, maybe that's where they're hiding now.'

'Wouldn't a stolen Land-Rover look a bit obvious in the city?' Hoody didn't jump to conclusions. 'Especially with a trailer and a pony. Where would they keep it?'

She shook her head. 'I don't know. But there would be places. There's lots of waste ground around, and empty buildings. Old factories, houses that are boarded up. They could easily hide a pony somewhere like that.' If she was right, if they really were about to narrow things down to one area of the city, there was room for hope. Carly glanced at Hoody's narrow expression. Obviously he didn't agree.

For the first time Trish looked up from her work. 'It might be worth phoning the police to tell them. What do you think?' she asked Sam.

The girl nodded, and as her boss went off to the house, she quietly praised Carly and Hoody for what they were trying to do. 'Every little bit of information helps,' she told them. 'Trish will want the police to prosecute these thieves, even if we don't get to Smudge in time.'

The last phrase sent Carly's rising hopes crashing. 'What do you mean?'

'Well, you know what usually happens to stolen ponies, don't you?' Sam cleared her throat and looked away.

'Yeah, we do.' Hoody cut her off. He jerked his head at Vinny, telling him it was time to go.

But Sam decided to spell it out. 'You've got to

face it, his chances aren't good. If these men have driven him back to the city, it'll be for only a little while, until – well – until, you know!'

'Until they find a pet food place that won't ask questions!' Carly exploded. The nightmare was back. She turned on her heel and ran.

They rode back to town in silence, along the long, straight City Road. Vinny sat tucked under Hoody's legs, as good as gold.

'Which bus would we have to catch for Sedgewood?' Carly asked. Traffic swirled around them as they wove through Fiveways, along underpasses, over curving bridges on concrete stilts.

Hoody shrugged. 'Number 62 from Beacon Street. Change at the Town Hall. Catch a number 40 out the other side to Sedgewood.' He looked out at the rain. 'I don't need to ask why.'

'You don't have to come if you don't want to.' For some reason, she kept on taking things out on Hoody, when really it was everyone, everything else that got in the way. Why was the bus so slow? Why did every traffic light have to be at red?

'Carly, it's like a needle in a haystack! Sedge-wood's massive. Where are we going to start?'

She could not only keep on using the facts they already had. It might not seem like much, but they had to keep on plugging away. 'City Farm,' she decided.

'What for? There's no way they'll have taken Smudge anywhere near there!'

'I know that.' She sat staring out through the trickles of rain on the window. 'Steve told me about Geoff Best. He's the manager who saw the thieves hanging about there last week, so he's the one we have to talk to now.'

'What's he going to tell us that we don't know already?' The more Carly ran headlong at things, the more Hoody wanted her to slow down. 'Listen, I can't believe it's me saying this, but don't you think we ought to check with your dad first?'

Surprise made her turn and stare. 'You want us to be sensible?' He was the one who never had a home to go to, who was always taking risks.

Hoody's face was bright red. 'Put it this way: let *me* get the bus out to Sedgewood. I'll have a scout around, while you let them know what's going on at Beech Hill.'

This was their stop at last. Carly stood up and pressed the bell. She hopped on to the greasy pavement, stood waiting for Hoody and Vinny, feeling the cool rain on her face.

'No way!' she told him. 'We *both* call in at my place, then we both go and see Geoff Best!'

For some reason, he grinned, then straightened his face. 'Deal,' he said.

Paul Grey was still in the operating theatre. There were two more patients on his list after he'd finished fixing a steel pin into an RTA cat's broken hip.

'I don't like the idea of you going to Sedge-wood at this time of day,' he told Carly. 'I think you should wait until morning.'

'But, Dad, it stays light till late. It's not dangerous.'

'What difference will a few hours make?'

'All the difference!' He knew the reason. But as she hovered in the prep room, waiting for his answer, she had a sinking feeling that the answer would be no.

'So why not talk to Geoff Best on the phone? Wouldn't that be just as good?' He drilled carefully into the hip bone with a fine electric drill. The two broken sections could be held together with a stainless steel pin. From the X-ray on the screen he could judge exactly where the pin should go.

Carly hesitated. She hadn't thought of the phone.

'And check with Steve before anyone goes dashing across town. See if he's heard any more from the police.' Paul picked up the tiny metal pin with a pair of forceps and edged it into place.

'OK,' she agreed reluctantly.

'Oh, and Carly, Liz was in here a couple of minutes ago, asking where you were. She said it was important.'

So she went to reception looking for Liz, to find Steve agreeing with Hoody to drive them across to Sedgewood in the van.

'No need for the bus,' he told him. 'Nelson's fit to go home, so I'm driving him back to the security firm who owns him. I have to go near City Farm in any case.'

'Great!' Hoody gladly accepted the lift. He turned to Carly. 'What did your dad say?'

'He said no. But if Steve takes us, he'll probably change his mind.' She retraced her steps, then bumped into Liz in the prep room.

'Carly!' The young vet was in a hurry. 'I need you!' She grabbed her jacket from behind the door, then scrawled a message on the whiteboard for Paul to read.

'What for?' Carly's head was in a whirl. She wanted to go to Sedgewood, but now Liz needed her help.

'Emergency call-out. Can you come?'

'Where to?' She tried to make out the hasty message.

'Worsley Common. Trish Clarke just rang.' Liz raced out, leaving the door swinging.

Carly stayed just long enough to read the words on the board: 'Phone call from the quarantine stables – condition of colt deteriorating. Will attend.'

Trish Clarke ran to open the gate as Liz and Carly arrived. They drove past a couple of patient journalists with cameras, who clicked into action and took flash photographs as the car slid into the yard.

'What's wrong now?' one of the newspapermen called. 'Why has she called you back?'

Liz ignored them and ran for Spider's stable. Sam stood at the door, anxiously waiting. 'Fetch another rug, a sponge and warm water,' Liz told Carly. 'We'll do what we can.'

'He can hardly breathe!' Sam went to the tack room with Carly. 'I checked him at half five and he was so bad we rang Liz straight off.'

They ran with the equipment, to find Liz in the stable with Trish. Both women knelt in the straw beside the patient. Liz was sounding his chest, Trish softly stroking his head.

'Double pneumonia,' Liz murmured. 'Probably a secondary infection. His lungs are inflamed, and that's closed up the tiny air spaces. See how shallow his breathing is!'

Carly went and gave Trish the warm sponge. The pony was sweating heavily, breathing fast in short, painful gasps. 'What can we do?' she pleaded with Liz.

'I'm giving him a different antibiotic to see if it works any better. The problem is, he can hardly get enough oxygen into his blood stream to keep his heart going!' She prepared the syringe and injected Spider's neck. 'When Trish has washed him down, we'll rug him and bandage his legs to keep him warm. Pneumonia makes him sweat a lot, but the cold is harmful too.'

Sam ran off to the tack room again, this time for leg bandages.

'Here, Carly, you rub with a dry towel once Trish has sponged him down.' Liz gave another instruction, leaned close and listened again to the inflamed lungs. She shook her head and went tight-lipped, helping Sam to fit the bandages around each leg.

Spider lay without moving, head back, struggling for each shallow breath. As they finished their work and gently placed the warm rug over him, he rolled his eyes and closed them.

Liz rocked back on to her heels and stood up. Trish and Sam knelt by his side. Carly saw the gasping sides shudder in and out, in and out as the pony lost consciousness. She swung round to face Liz, waiting to hear what they should do next.

'That's it,' Liz said quietly.

Spider drew one last breath. Then his sides stopped heaving, his eyes stayed closed. He was dead.

7

Liz and Carly stayed at Worsley Common to nurse Minty and Ginger until late that night.

Under the glare of a bare electric bulb they steamed the ponies and rubbed down their shaking, sweating bodies. They smeared their nostrils with Vaseline and fomented their swollen glands with a solution of hot water and epsom salts to bring the painful abscesses to a head, ready for lancing.

'Check Minty's hind legs while we have her standing up.' Liz told Carly to look for new swellings. 'I'm hoping there won't be any because we managed to start her course of antibiotics sooner than we did with Spider.'

Anxiously Carly ran her hand up and down the pony's trembling legs. 'I can't feel anything.'

'Good.' Liz unstrapped the steaming feed bag, then went outside into the dark yard to tip the hay onto a smouldering fire. 'Bedtime,' she told the pony when she came back, slinging a rug over her back and leaving Carly to fasten the girth strap.

Carly soothed and petted her as she bedded her down. 'Sleep well,' she urged as the pony went down on her bandaged knees and rolled stiffly on to her side in the bed of straw. 'You'll feel better in the morning, wait and see!'

Minty breathed heavily and shook her head. Carly pushed her long white mane out of her eyes, then stroked her neck. She backed out of the stall, closed the door and turned out the light.

'I've settled Ginger for the night.' Liz met her in the yard. Ignoring the persistent cameramen still hanging about by the gate, she put her hands on her hips and gazed up at the sky. The drizzle had eased and the clouds cleared. Now there was a sprinkling of stars and a thin crescent moon. 'He's a tough old thing, so he's holding his own.'

In the darkness they both thought of Spider.

Then Trish called them into the house for a cup of tea. Relieved that this time she wasn't angry with them about the colt's death, Liz accepted.

'Maybe, with a bit of luck, those journalists will give up and go to the pub,' she sighed. 'I don't fancy facing their questions at this time of night.' She took a mug from Trish and handed it to Carly.

'No chance.' Trish peered out through the curtains. 'They're still there. They know a good story.' She imagined tomorrow's headline news. ' "Killer Disease Claims First Victim!"'

Carly sipped her tea. Trish's kitchen was light and cosy, with an old-fashioned tiled floor and a big pine table around which they sat after their tiring evening's work. She noticed red, blue and yellow rosettes pinned along the heavy ceiling beams: prizes won by Trish's ponies in competitions. There were silver cups on the shelves, and framed photos of ponies and riders on the walls.

'We could stay here overnight if you like,' Liz suggested. 'I carry a couple of sleeping bags in the car. We could keep an eye on Minty and Ginger; take it in turns.'

Trish gave an exhausted, embarrassed smile. 'Thanks, I'd be very grateful. Especially considering the way I've treated you.' She reminded them of how she'd blamed Liz for not picking up the disease straight away.

That seems like weeks ago, Carly thought, through a tired haze. She clasped the warm mug and let her thoughts drift.

'It's OK, I understand.' The young vet was glad that Trish didn't blame her any more. 'It must have looked like I didn't know what I was doing. But strangles is rare these days. A lot of people have their horses vaccinated against it, especially if it's known to be in the area.'

'But it wasn't, that's the problem. Not until Mrs Mitchell brought Minty along.' She put a hand over her eyes and rubbed her forehead. 'She's on the phone all the time, asking me how Minty is, telling me Julia is worried sick.'

'At least Steve's report is going to say you weren't to blame. That's one good thing.'

'One little speck of light at the end of a very dark tunnel,' Trish agreed. 'Tomorrow was the day when the team from the Lottery fund was due to visit. I had to cancel, of course.' She dragged herself to her feet to show Liz the spare room where she and Carly could sleep.

The two women were upstairs when the phone rang in the hall.

'Could you answer that?' Trish called down to Carly. 'If it's Mrs Mitchell, say that Minty's still holding her own!'

Gingerly Carly picked up the phone, expecting a woman's frantic voice. 'Hello?'

'Carly?' Paul Grey sounded as surprised as she was.

'Yes, it's me.'

'I expected Trish to answer. How are things?'

'Spider died.' Her own voice sounded odd as she told him.

'Yes, I heard. Trish rang Steve to tell him. I'm sorry, love.'

'But we think Minty and Ginger will be OK.'

'That's good. Hoody's here. Can you tell him the latest?'

She waited while her dad handed over the phone. 'Hi, Hoody.'

'Hi. Sorry about Spider.'

'Thanks. Listen, it's not going to happen to Ginger as well!' She wanted him to believe her. 'We're stopping over to nurse him and Minty. What are you doing at Beech Hill anyway?'

'Waiting for you. Listen: me and Steve, we took Nelson home. He's OK. He was glad to be back. He lives in a kennels behind a railway station with five other guard dogs. Steve knows the man who runs the place, says they're well looked after.'

'That's great. What about City Farm? Did you go there?' The emergency with Spider had filled her head. Now she needed to catch up.

'That's what I wanted to tell you about. We saw Geoff Best—'

'Did you ask him about the men?'

'Hang on. Yeah, we did. The police had been to ask him the same questions. He told us what he told them: one guy is over six feet tall with a moustache, not much hair on top. The kid he was with fits the description you gave. And the police now think they know who they're looking for. The older one's been in loads of trouble with them for nicking things from farms and big country gardens. He lives on an estate on the edge of Sedgewood.'

'It's the same men, then?' She'd been right about the connection between Smudge and Nelson.

'For sure. Geoff gave us a couple of places in the area where they might hang out with a stolen trailer, so we went and looked. We tried some old railway sidings with a row of empty brick huts, then some wrecked allotments across the track. Nothing. Bad news.'

Carly wasn't surprised. She could tell by Hoody's voice that they hadn't had any luck. 'We can try again tomorrow, when I get back,' she insisted.

'Do you want the good news?'

'Is there any?' Her legs and back ached with the effort of nursing the ponies, and there was a dull ache in her heart over Spider.

'Steve had the idea to ring the slaughterhouses. He gave them Smudge's serial number and they checked their lists. What I'm trying to say is that they all came back and said the same thing: no black-and-white freeze-marked ponies have gone through their place in the last couple of days!'

Carly gripped the phone. 'So Smudge is still alive?'

'We hope!' Hoody said. 'Anyway, one thing's for sure: they needn't think we're about to give up now!'

'Both infected ponies made it through the night,' Liz told the journalists at the gate.

Carly had waded through a shallow tray of disinfected water to hold the gate open as Liz drove through, but the three men had stepped in front of the car, barring her way.

'What are their chances now?' one asked, pen poised over his notepad.

'Fifty-fifty,' Liz muttered, waiting for Carly to close the gate and hop in. 'Look, if you don't mind, we've to get back to Beech Hill. We've got a clinic in half an hour!'

'Have there been any more cases identified among the other ponies in the field?' The journalists stood their ground. 'Is there any news on the one that was stolen?'

'No, and no.' She was firm as she edged the car forward. 'Let me through, please.'

One of the men backed into a post that displayed a KEEP OUT! notice. He pushed it to one side and ran alongside the little sports car. 'Is there any truth in the rumour that Trish Clarke is having a nervous breakdown over this?'

'No!' Liz revved the engine hard, ready to leave him standing. 'This is too much!' she complained.

They'd left the stable owner to cope with looking after Minty and Ginger single-handed until Sam arrived at half past eight. She was OK, she'd assured them. She'd snatched some sleep during the night, thanks to Liz and Carly, and was ready to face another nerve-wracking day.

'Hang on, there's a car coming,' Carly warned. Their getaway was ruined. As Liz put on the brake, a large silver four-wheel drive cruised down the lane towards them.

'I know that car!' Carly warned, even before it drew to a halt and a dark-haired woman climbed down. 'It's Mrs Mitchell!'

'What does she want?' Liz got out of the car and slammed the door. She was tired, and Mrs Mitchell's constant phone calls had worn down her patience. She strode across to intercept the woman before she reached the gate.

Carly followed. She could hear Liz telling Minty's owner that the quarantine rules were still in force. *What's the point?* she wondered. Mrs Mitchell knew that already. She glimpsed the daughter, Julia, huddled miserably inside the car.

'Don't worry, I haven't come to pester Trish,' Mrs Mitchell said. 'Quite the opposite, as a matter of fact.' Her pretty face with its dark brown eyes and arched eyebrows was creased into a frown. 'I want to take the pressure off her.'

'How?' Liz looked doubtful.

Glancing across the yard, over the shoulders of the three eager journalists, Carly saw Trish emerge from Minty's stable. When she saw her visitors, she stopped in her tracks then came slowly across.

'Trish, it's Kate Mitchell!' She pushed through to the gate. 'It's all right, I don't want to come in.'

'You can't, in any case.' Trish pointed to the wobbly sign, the disinfectant dip, the low fire smouldering in the background.

'I wanted to come and tell you this in person!' Kate Mitchell rushed on. She looked at the journalists. 'And I want you people to write it down!'

The journalists didn't wait to be told. They'd already spotted an interesting development.

They stood, pencils at the ready.

'I need to say in public, in person, that this is all my fault!' Minty's owner made her announcement.

The newspapermen scribbled. A camera clicked.

'That's right. I'm ashamed to admit it, but I've been talking to my own vet. He confirmed what you've always said: that Minty could easily have caught strangles before we brought her to Worsley Common! In other words, we brought the illness with us!'

Carly saw Trish nod her head, then give a short, hollow laugh. She turned to trudge back towards the stable.

'No, don't go. I mean to put it right!'

'How can you do that?' Liz stepped in. 'You made Trish take the blame, and that's the story that's been put out on the news. It's just about ruined her.'

Mrs Mitchell nodded and called Trish back again. 'I'm sorry, I didn't know what I was saying at the time. It was Julia who brought me to my senses yesterday. She told me Minty was already off-colour before we left home. She made me call our vet. He came with a lab technician to take samples from Minty's stable. They made us burn all her bedding afterwards. What's more, they expect to find the virus when they do the tests!'

The three journalists could hardly scribble fast enough. Carly watched them fill their pages with shorthand squiggles and curves. The evening papers would carry sensational new headlines: 'Fresh Source For Strangles Epidemic!' 'Riding School Owner Not To Blame!'

More questions and answers shot back and forth. 'What did Mrs Mitchell think of the care that had been given to Minty since she fell ill at Worsley Common?' 'Excellent. Everyone had worked tirelessly to pull the pony through.' 'Was Mrs Mitchell definitely withdrawing all her early claims that Worsley Common was to blame?' 'Categorically, yes!'

As Trish and Liz listened in stunned silence, Carly walked slowly towards the giant silver car. She looked up at the strained, pale face of Julia Mitchell.

The girl looked down. There were dark shadows under her eyes, her bottom lip trembled.

'Thanks,' Carly said softly.

She nodded stiffly. 'How's Minty?' she whispered.

'Weak, but fighting back. Liz says we'll know by the end of today whether or not the infection is going to spread.'

Another nod. 'Thanks.' This time, though Julia Mitchell bit her lip and tried to turn away, Carly saw two large tears spill and roll down her pale cheeks.

8

'So, the pressure's off Trish Clarke!' Paul Grey picked up the evening newspaper after a busy afternoon clinic. He had his feet up on the desk in the office, taking ten minutes off before he and Liz got down to some paperwork.

'She deserves a break.' Liz read the headline: ' "Not Guilty! Riding School Owner Cleared Of Spreading Killer Disease." It wouldn't surprise me if she could actually sue the Mitchells for bringing the disease to Worsley Common, instead of the other way round.'

'The article praises you as well,' Paul pointed

out. 'There's a quote from Trish saying it's thanks to you that more ponies haven't died.'

Liz blushed. 'And to Carly. I hope it mentions her.'

'Yep.' He grinned and pushed the paper across the desk. 'Carly, would you like to see your name in print?'

'No thanks.' It was too embarrassing. And too soon to put the whole crisis behind them. After all, one pony had died, and the stables were still contagious.

'Here, give it to me!' Before she could stop him, Hoody seized it. 'Hey, they spelt your name wrong! Twice! "Carli" with an "i" and "Gray" with an "a"! And how old are you?'

'Stop it, Hoody!' She tried to snatch the paper back.

'They say you're only eleven!' he crowed. ' "Eleven-year-old vet's daughter, Carli Gray, stayed at Worsley Common all night helping super-vet Liz Hutchins nurse the ponies through the worst of the crisis!"' He stabbed his finger at the crumpled page. 'They've even got a photo-graph!'

'Let's see!' At last she grabbed it and studied

the picture of a girl with dark, curly hair, a pointed face and staring eyes. 'That isn't me! I look about eight!'

'It is you. They've printed your name under it.' Hoody made the most of her stuttering dismay. He followed her out of the office into reception, chased by an excited Vinny.

'Can I have a bit of hush!' Steve warned, putting his hand over the phone.

'Ssh!' Bupinda repeated. 'It's Geoff Best from the City Farm.'

Carly and Hoody stopped fooling around to listen.

'OK, Geoff, I've got that. Which bit of wasteland did he mean? The old car plant. Yep, got it!' Steve hung up and scribbled something on a pad.

'Is it to do with the men who took Smudge?' Carly asked. She'd picked up the sudden tension in Steve's voice.

'Could be. It's long shot, but Geoff thought it was worth ringing me.' Steve put on his jacket and took the van keys out of his pocket. 'Nelson's owner, Winston Greenaway, just rang Geoff to tell him that he'd been walking the dogs on some wasteland behind the railway sidings.'

'We went there last night!' Hoody said. 'We never found anything.'

'No, this is further back, on the site of an old car factory. It covers a massive area, all empty and run down. Winston often takes his dogs there for a run, apparently. Anyway, the point is, he took Nelson, and everything was OK, until suddenly the dog started behaving strangely around a row of disused workshops. Winston didn't get what was going on: Nelson bared his teeth and growled, started to bark at nothing. He ran out of control, so Winston got him on the lead and took him straight back home. It was only when he got there and managed to quieten the dog down that he thought it might mean something.'

'So he rang Geoff?' Hoody followed Steve out to the van with Vinny at his heels. 'And Geoff rang you?'

He nodded. 'Do you want to come and take a look this time?' he asked Carly.

She jumped in the back without a word, slammed the door and held on tight as Steve swung out on to Beech Hill.

'It could be nothing, remember.' He wove

through the traffic on to City Road and along the series of tunnels that passed under the heart of the city. 'A false alarm. Don't build up your hopes.'

'But Nelson wouldn't bark for nothing.' Hoody knew he was a well-trained guard dog.

'It could be a result of being attacked last week,' Steve warned. 'It's probably made him edgy. Anything could have set him off.'

The city motorway took them out into an inner city jungle of tower blocks, old churches and run-down shops. Peering though the back window, holding on to Vinny, Carly noticed a sign which read 'H.M. Prison, Sedgewood Green' in front of a grim fortress-style building with giant double gates and a round tower to either side. Then another row of shops, a British Rail sign outside a station. They passed it and stopped at traffic lights.

'Not long now,' Hoody said from the front passenger seat.

They swung off the main road into a maze of sidestreets.

'I'm going to call at Winston's place, see if we can borrow Nelson for a while,' Steve explained.

He stopped the van outside a modern office. Carly and Hoody watched him speak to a woman on the desk then go through a door in the back. He came out a couple of minutes later with a tall man dressed in a white shirt with a bright orange and yellow tie. The man held Nelson on a lead as he brought him out under the Greenaway Security sign above the door.

'That's Mr Greenaway,' Hoody whispered. 'It looks like he said yes.'

Steve took the Rottweiler and put him in the back of the van with Carly and Vinny. Hoody's dog recognised an old friend, complete with scars. As Nelson bounded up, they ducked and sniffed at one another, tails wagging.

Winston Greenaway smiled in and nodded. 'You look after my dog, you hear!' he told them, as he closed the door and waved them off.

Then it was only a short drive to the deserted car factory, with its acres of broken tarmac. Weeds grew in the gaps and block after block of brick assembly sheds stood empty.

Steve pulled up by a tall metal fence and went and rattled at a locked gate. Then they cruised around the outside of the wasteland, looking in on lumps of twisted metal and oily engine parts, heaps of old tyres. From inside the van Nelson caught sight of where they were and let out a loud bark.

'Where to now?' Carly muttered. She had hold of the Rottweiler's collar, trying to calm him. His bark had nearly shattered her eardrums.

'Let's try round the back.' Steve drove down the side of the site, along a road lined with old workshops. A train thundered past at the end of the cul-de-sac, windows gleaming in the evening sun. Vinny and Nelson barked at the sudden din.

'I'm going to take a look.' Steve drew up next to a pile of rubble and rusty metal girders. 'Winston mentioned these workshops. This was where Nelson started acting up.' He opened the back doors to let both dogs out.

Vinny bounded out and shot off to explore. But Carly had to coax Nelson to come with them. 'It's OK,' she told him. 'Nothing's going to happen to you.' She eased him out and kept him on the lead, frowning at Hoody. 'Are you like me? Do you get a bad feeling about this place?'

He nodded and they looked round cautiously. To one side the old car factory carpark stretched down to the rail track. To the other was the ramshackle collection of disused workshops, all boarded up, with parts of the roofs missing and piles of filthy rubble dumped outside. This was where Vinny had made for. Carly spotted him down a narrow alley between two workshops, nose to the ground, his long, thin tail wagging eagerly. 'Come on, Nelson!' She wanted them to follow Hoody's dog.

At first the Rottweiler pulled back, then he let her lead him on. Hoody and Steve had gone to investigate other alleyways and dark corners. She could hear them opening nearby doors, their footsteps echoing. Ahead of her, just out of sight, Vinny barked.

Nelson dug in his heels. He started to growl and his hackles rose.

'What is it?' Carly peered down the narrow space between two derelict workshops. Something had spooked him again. She looked more closely. There was a yard behind the workshops, a smell of diesel oil, the glint of a shiny new metal roof on some kind of vehicle parked there. She gasped.

Then Vinny came hurtling back down the

alleyway, barking at her to come. He turned and ran ahead, disappeared into the hidden yard.

'Hoody! Steve!' Carly called. 'Over here!' She followed slowly, coaxing Nelson along. His growl came from deep in his throat; a rumbling warning.

There was a barrier at the end of the alley; a sheet of corrugated metal shoved upright as a kind of makeshift gate. But there was a gap to squeeze through. Carly sent Nelson ahead after Vinny. Had the others heard her call? She glanced over her shoulder, then crept through the gap.

And she found what they were looking for. There in the overgrown yard stood the stolen trailer. The ramp was down, wisps of straw were scattered against the double doors of an old lock-up garage. Vinny raced up the ramp, his bark echoing.

'Steve! Hoody!' She yelled again. Nelson strained at the lead. 'We've found the trailer! Ring the police, quick!'

As she let the Rottweiler off the lead, Hoody came running. 'Where's the pony? Did you find him?' He took in the scene, ran to each corner of the yard, looking for more clues.

'I don't know. Maybe he's in here!' Carly followed Nelson. The dog had his nose to the ground, snuffling at the door of the lock-up. 'They must have hidden Smudge behind here!' She tried the handle, but it wouldn't turn. 'It's locked!'

As Hoody seized it and tried to wrench the doors open, Steve appeared. He slid his mobile phone into his pocket and told them to stand back. 'OK, the police are on their way. Let's just take it easy!'

'Listen!' Carly had heard noises from inside the garage. Hard hooves clattered on concrete, there was a high, wild whinny of a frightened pony. 'It's Smudge!'

'He's alive.' Hoody stood back from the door and quietened Vinny. 'We got here in time.'

But it wasn't over yet; they still had to get the pony out. 'What if the men come back?' Carly ran to the road, looked up and down. There was no sign of the Land-Rover. 'What are we going to do?'

'Smash the lock,' Steve decided. He looked round for a stone heavy enough to do the job, found one and told the others to stand back. He lifted the stone above his head and brought it crashing down on to the handle: once, twice, three times.

Inside the garage, they could hear Smudge rear and squeal.

Finally the handle gave way and the doors swung open.

At first it was too dark inside for Carly to see. Then she made out the black-and-white pony cowering in the corner. He was cruelly tethered on a short rope, rearing and pulling in panic, his hooves rattling on the bare concrete. The sight made her cry out angrily.

But Steve kept calm. He waited for Smudge to settle before he moved in, told Carly and Hoody to take the dogs on to the street and keep a look-out for the police. 'Leave this to me,' he insisted.

So they forced themselves away from Smudge's dark prison and went to wait by the kerb. Hoody leaned against a pile of old tyres, arms folded. Carly bent to stroke and praise Vinny and Nelson in turn.

'Did it look like he'd got this strangles thing?' Hoody asked. It seemed to be taking an age for Steve to lead Smudge to safety.

Carly shook her head. 'I don't think so. He'd be weak and shivery if he had. I think he was just scared.'

'So what did they plan to do with him? They couldn't leave him locked up in there forever.'

'Who knows? I suppose in the end, when the fuss had died down, they could just have dumped him. Or left him here to starve!' Carly heard a car coming down the road. She stepped out on to the pavement, expecting the bright orange stripe and blue light of a police car.

But her heart thudded in her chest. It was a Land-Rover – *the* Land-Rover. At the moment she realised who it was and what it meant, the driver saw them. He must have only had time to take in a girl and a boy, two dogs. One of the dogs, the Rottweiler who the thieves knew of old, opened its mouth and bared its teeth. Then it launched itself at the oncoming car.

'Nelson, no!' Carly screamed.

The dog charged the Land-Rover. The car drove straight at him. At the last second, Nelson swerved to one side, wheeled round and charged again.

'They're trying to run him down!' Hoody was

on his feet, in the middle of the road, calling for the car to stop.

'They'll kill him!' Frantically Carly hung on to Vinny to stop him from following.

Nelson ran snarling at the car. The driver didn't even brake. He didn't care if he hit the dog, he wouldn't let anything get in the way. He kept on coming.

'We've got to stop him!' Carly yelled.

She did the only thing she could think of to save Nelson from going under the wheels of the Land-Rover. She took an old tyre from the pile behind Hoody, swung it round and flung it like a giant frisbee right in the path of the car. Then another. Then Hoody joined in, taking tyres from the heap and flinging them into the road.

The car hit one and veered sideways. As Nelson charged again from the far side, the driver swerved. He hit another tyre, sent it careering down the road.

And still Hoody and Carly kept on blocking the Land-Rover's path with more tyres, forcing it off the road. They saw the driver wrench the steering wheel, watched the fair-haired passenger cling on as the car swerved and tilted.

Brave Nelson charged, darting clear at the last moment. Brakes squealed, but it was too late: the car shot out of control on to the pavement.

Metal scraped and crunched against brick. The front end of the car folded like paper as it hit the wall. Carly grabbed Nelson and closed her eyes.

Silence. Then the wail of a siren, a flashing blue light. Carly knelt on the ground amongst the tumbling, rolling tyres.

They'd done it; everyone was safe! She opened her eyes, put her arms around Nelson and hugged him for dear life.

9

It was on TV on the early evening news: 'Two men from the Sedgewood area have been arrested for the theft of a pony from a disease-stricken riding school at Worsley Common. The arrest followed an incident involving a stolen Land-Rover and a guard dog owned by Greenaway Security. No one was hurt.'

Film showed the scene of the arrest, with the crashed Land-Rover and car tyres scattered across the road.

'Police have named the men as Derek Ritchie, aged 38, and Sean Bradley, aged 20, both from

Sedgewood. The arrest came after local animal inspector, Steve Winter, traced the pony to derelict land close to a disused car plant. He and his young helpers, Carly Grey and Jon Hood, plan to return the pony, who has been declared fit and well after his ordeal, to his relieved owner later this evening.'

Hoody was only ever called Hoody. He cringed at the use of his first name. 'Who told them that?' he hissed.

'Come on, you two, it's getting dark.' Paul Grey didn't give them a chance to get big-headed. He was sending Liz out ahead of Steve, who would tow the trailer to Worsley Common. 'Time to get a move on if you want to go too.'

Carly flicked the TV off. 'Aren't you coming?' she asked her dad.

He shook his head. 'This is Liz's case.' They'd checked the pony for injury together after he'd been brought to Beech Hill. Now that he was declared fit, Paul was happy to hand over to his assistant. 'But if you go, you can get a progress report on Minty and Ginger.'

So they hopped in the van for what they hoped would be the last time that day. The excitement of finding Smudge, the drama of the arrest, then interviews with the police had made a long and tiring afternoon. But Carly wouldn't dream of missing this bit. As they towed the trailer out of town, she pictured the look on Trish Clarke's face when they returned Smudge to his field.

'Welcome home!' Trish leaned on the fence and beamed. Smudge teetered down the ramp on to the lush green grass, took one look round and trotted to join the group of ponies standing under a tree at the far side of the field.

Carly and Hoody enjoyed the sight. Light was fading, the clouds were tinged with gold over Minster Woods. The ponies greeted Smudge with tossing manes and stamping feet.

'The other good news is that all your ponies except Minty and Ginger can be declared free of disease,' Liz told Trish. 'And even those two won't be infectious for many more days, so it shouldn't be long before we can have the quarantine notices lifted and you can get back to normal.'

Trish nodded slowly. 'Things are looking up. I heard from the Lottery people today. They tell me they're still considering us for a grant after all.'

'That's brilliant!'

'I suspect Kate Mitchell had something to do with it. I gather she made sure they realised where the infection had started. She's busy taking all the blame, and apparently singing our praises for the way we've nursed Minty for them.'

'Quite right too.' Liz rested against the fence, soaking in the peaceful scene, as Carly and Hoody went to help Steve bolt the ramp into place and back the trailer out of the field.

'Are you coming or staying?' he asked them. He wanted to head back to town to take the trailer to the police compound.

'Staying. We'll get a lift back with Liz, thanks.' Carly and Hoody wanted to look in on Minty and Ginger.

They strolled across the yard together, then split off – Hoody towards Ginger's stable, Carly to visit Minty, while Liz and Trish saw Steve off down the lane.

'Steady on, I haven't got anything for you!' Hoody protested, as the old rascal thrust his head over the door and pushed his nose against Hoody's chest. 'No doggy chocs! Hey, watch it!'

Carly smiled. Ginger must be feeling a lot better. She opened the door and stepped inside Minty's stable, expecting to find her on the road to recovery too.

But the grey pony was in terrible trouble. She was down on her knees inside her stall, struggling to get up. Too weak to stand, her legs kept collapsing under her. Then she would struggle again, letting her head sink to the ground as she tried to suck in air, then lifting it and trying to force herself upright.

Carly ran to her. She supported Minty's head, heard the rasping breaths, held back her own panic. 'Hoody, fetch Liz quick!' she shouted, her hand on the pony's quivering neck to calm her. 'Steady,' she whispered. It was pathetic to see her struggling for breath, weakening with every passing second.

Just like poor Spider! Carly knelt helpless in the dark, feeling the pony's life ebb away.

Then Liz came running, clutching her vet's bag, with Trish and Hoody crowding in behind.

'Put the light on!' She took in the situation in a

flash, took out her stethoscope and sounded Minty's chest. Then she felt for a pulse.

'What is it? Pneumonia again?' Carly waited for the diagnosis. *Don't let her die*! she pleaded silently. *Not now; not after all this*!

Liz shook her head. 'No, this is pleurisy. It's a bacterial infection, but not quite the same.' She glanced up, noticed Hoody standing in the doorway. 'Run to the car and fetch my phone,' she told him.

'What can you do?' Carly still stroked Minty's neck.

'I'm not sure yet. This is a bad case.' Liz explained what was happening. 'It's not the air sacs inside the lungs that are inflamed this time, it's the outer membrane. There's a lining that covers the lungs, and there's supposed to be a gap between that and the lining of the chest. With pleurisy, the membranes get inflamed and the space fills up with fluid.'

Carly nodded. 'So why can't she breathe?'

'The fluid has built up and is pressing on the lungs. It's like squeezing air out of a balloon, and until the pressure eases, she can't suck enough air back in.'

By this time, Hoody had come back with the phone. 'What do you want it for?'

'I need to speak to Paul.' Quickly she punched in the numbers. 'There's a surgical procedure I can perform. I know in theory what happens, but this is the first time I've ever actually had to do it!'

'Hurry!' Trish urged. She could see Minty growing weaker and weaker.

'We're going to try and drain the fluid away,' Liz explained, still waiting for Carly's father to answer the phone. Every second seemed like an age. Then she heard his voice. 'Paul, Liz here. I need you to talk me through something, OK?' Quickly she described the emergency, then handed the phone to Carly. 'We're going to tap the fluid out of Minty's chest. Your dad is going to relay the instructions through you. You listen carefully to what he says, then you tell me.'

Carly put the phone to her ear. Her head swam in confusion. Would she be able to do this? Would it work?

'Carly, stay calm and listen closely, OK?' He spoke clearly and slowly.

'OK!' Yes, she could do it. Her dad would

explain it one step at a time. All she needed to do was repeat it. She watched Liz put on a pair of surgical gloves and unwrap a thin, pointed sterile steel tube which she attached to a wider plastic one.

'Tell him I've assembled the trocar,' Liz said. 'I'm giving Minty a local anaesthetic first, then we can begin.' She got to work to numb an area on the underside of Minty's chest. 'OK, ready.'

'Ready, Dad!'

'First, she has to make a cut two centimetres behind the elbow and level with it. Exactly two centimetres. Got that?'

Carly repeated it word for word. She sensed Hoody wince and take a step back as Liz measured and made the cut.

'Now she can insert the tube. She has to push it straight to avoid the ribs. Tell her not to put it in at a slant.'

Again Carly reported what he said.

'Is the pony struggling?' Paul Grey asked.

'No, she's too weak.' Minty's breath was so shallow they could hardly see her ribs rising and falling.

'If Liz manages to get it in straight, the trocar

will pierce the lining of the chest, then the fluid will begin to trickle out of the tube. Get ready for that,' her dad warned.

Carly told Liz. They waited as the tube went deep into the pony's flesh. Blood oozed from the wound. More seconds ticked by.

'You'll need something to catch the fluid,' Paul said.

'A bucket?' She caught sight of one hanging from a hook on the wall.

'That'll do. Is anything happening?'

'Not yet.'

Liz leaned forward, pressing the trocar carefully through a gap between the ribs. Then suddenly, the clear tube began to fill quickly with liquid. Trish moved in with a bucket to catch it as it flowed out of Minty's chest.

'She did it!' Carly gave a huge sigh, watched the pony's rib cage shudder and saw the lungs fill with air. 'It's working! Dad, Minty's breathing!'

'Well done. Tell Liz to leave the tube in place. I'm leaving Beech Hill right now. I'll be there as soon as I can!'

'Brilliant!' Hoody whispered, peering over

Carly's shoulder. 'And here's me thinking she was going to die!'

'Me too.'

Then they gazed in silence. Still the fluid drained into the bucket; so much that they could hardly believe it. Liz was kneeling back, watching the pony's lungs fill with air, leaning forward again to sound her chest and take her pulse. She counted silently, then looked up at Trish and nodded. 'Crisis over,' she said quietly.

A week later, on the last morning of the school holidays, Carly and Hoody went back to Worsley Common to see the men from the Ministry take down the quarantine notices.

'*Now* I believe it,' Trish told Liz. 'Now I can really relax!'

The men tossed the signs into the back of their pick-up and drove off. The riding school could open for business again.

'I'd better start cleaning the tack, then.' Sam got to work on the saddles and bridles, determined to make the leather gleam once more.

'And I'd better confirm with the special school that their lesson can go ahead as planned this afternoon.' Trish went whistling into the house to make her phone call.

'What about you two?' Liz asked Hoody and Carly. 'Do you want to come or stay?' She had a busy surgery to go back to after she'd run one last check on Ginger and Minty. Both ponies were back in the field with the others, slowly recovering from their ordeal. In a day or two, Minty would go home to the Mitchells.

'Stay!' Carly jumped in. She wanted to learn more about hocks and cannon bones, seedy toe and laminitis. *The Anatomy of the Horse* had become her favourite bedtime reading.

'Come!' Hoody had heard and seen enough. He reckoned that bits and snaffles bored him. Now that he knew that Ginger and Minty were going to be OK, he wanted to be back on the city streets, enjoying his last day of freedom.

But Vinny barked and ran into the field to play. He fetched a stick and dropped it at Hoody's feet, waiting for him to join in.

Carly grinned. 'He likes it here.'

'I don't.' Grudgingly Hoody picked up the stick and threw it. Vinny chased, caught up with it and rolled over. He trotted back, stick in mouth, to begin again. 'I get hay fever, remember.'

'Hoody, I've never heard you sneeze once!' she challenged. He could go back home if he liked, but Carly was set on helping Sam and Trish.

'Aaa – tchoo!'

'Very funny.'

'OK, Hoody comes, Carly stays,' Liz said briskly. 'What about Vinny?'

'Comes!'

'Stays!' they said.

'Aatchoo!' Hoody sneezed, for real this time. '*Whad-did-I-dell-you!*' he moaned through a blocked nose.

Vinny charged back with the stick, raising clouds of pollen as he came. A couple of ponies followed him, nostrils twitching, ears pricked.

'Here comes Ginger.' Carly pointed him out.

The sturdy pony came trotting to the fence. He poked his long face at Hoody and snuffled in his pocket for doggy chocs. When Hoody tried to back off, Ginger grabbed his T-shirt between strong yellow teeth.

'Looks like you're staying!' Liz laughed.

'*Oh, danks. Dat's great!*' Hoody tugged in vain.

Carly left them to it. She climbed the fence and

jumped into the field, wandered through silky grass, buttercups and daisies.

When she saw Minty split from the group and walk stiffly towards her, head swaying, white mane flopping over her dark brown eyes, she stopped to wait. Screwing her eyes up against the sun, she smiled and sighed. Right now, right here, enjoying Minty's recovery, Carly knew that this was exactly where she wanted to be.